Trace
Craze
WORKBOOKS

This workbook is suitable for Pre-K and K.
Instruct students to trace inside the letters with colored markers, crayons or pencils.

Credits
The fonts used in producing this workbook are a licensed product from Educational Fontware, Inc.
Freepik graphics used under premium licence.

For questions, comments or ideas please contact the author at: hellovictoriavita@gmail.com

ISBN-13: 9781730950513

Airplane

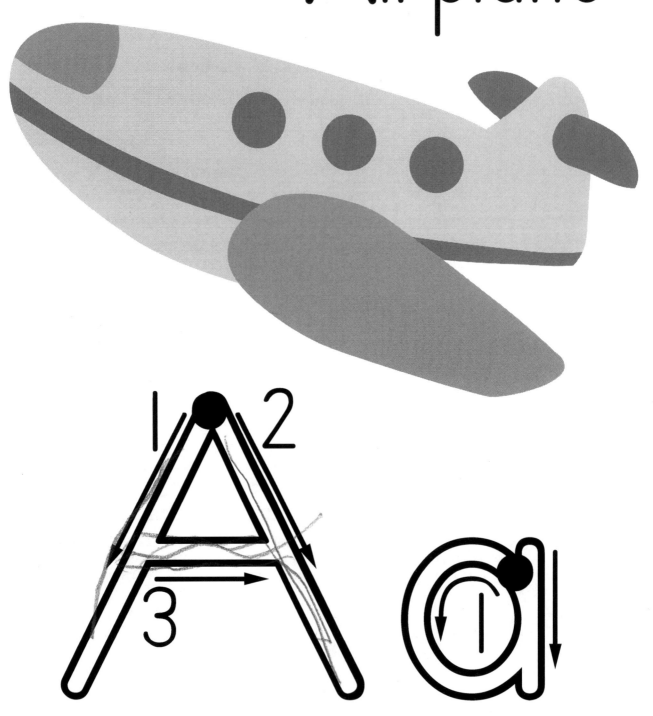

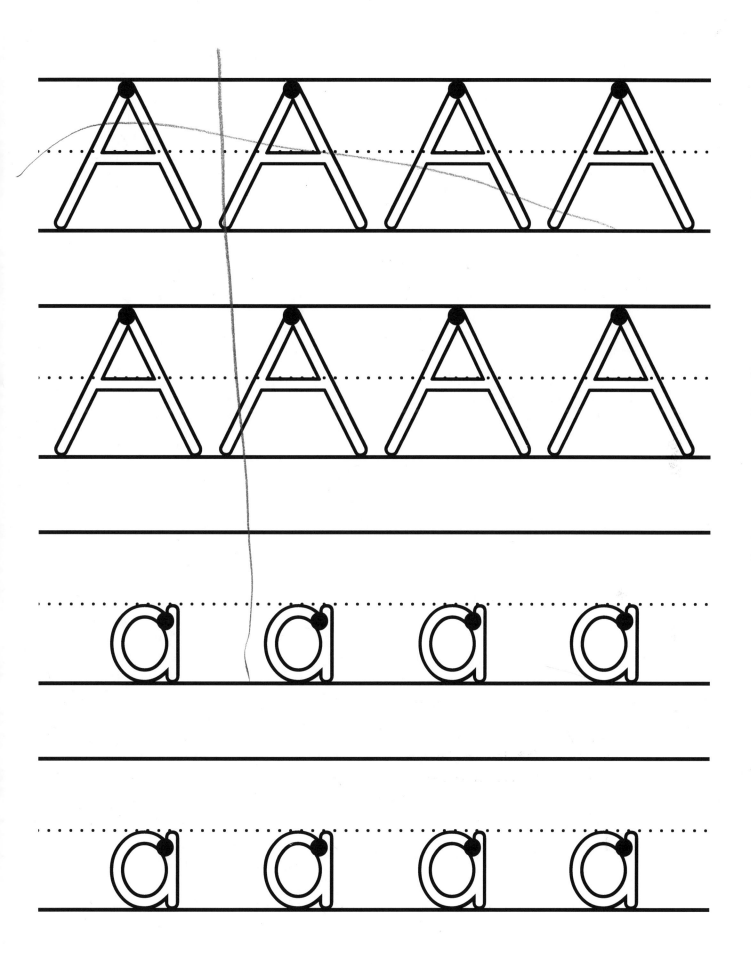

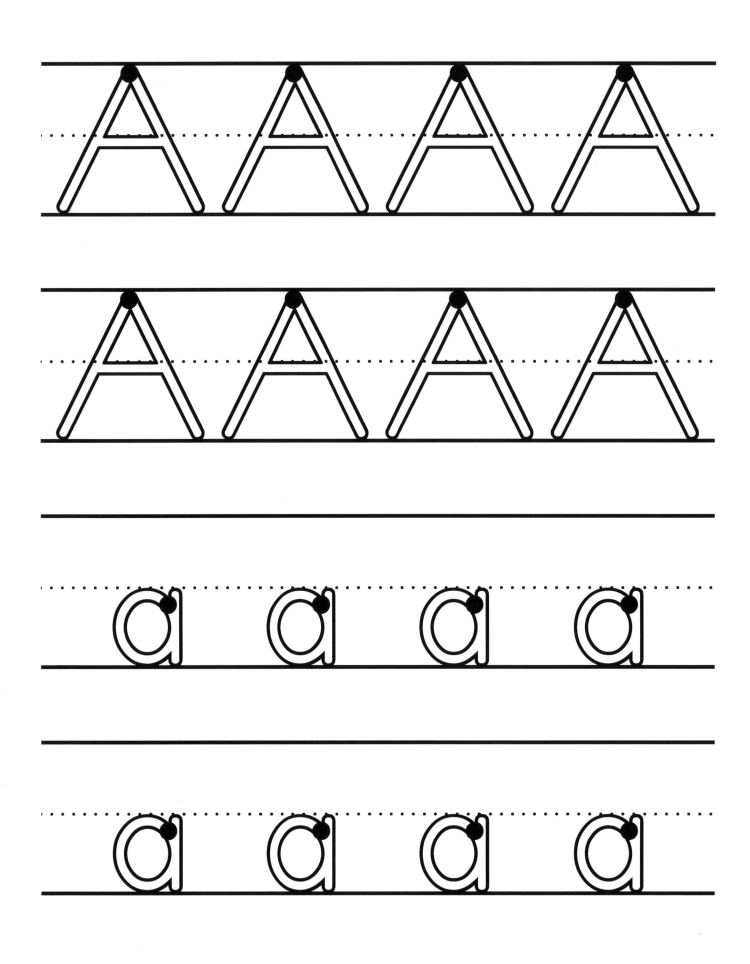

A

a

Boat

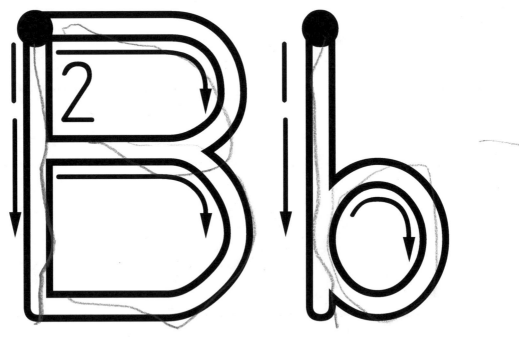

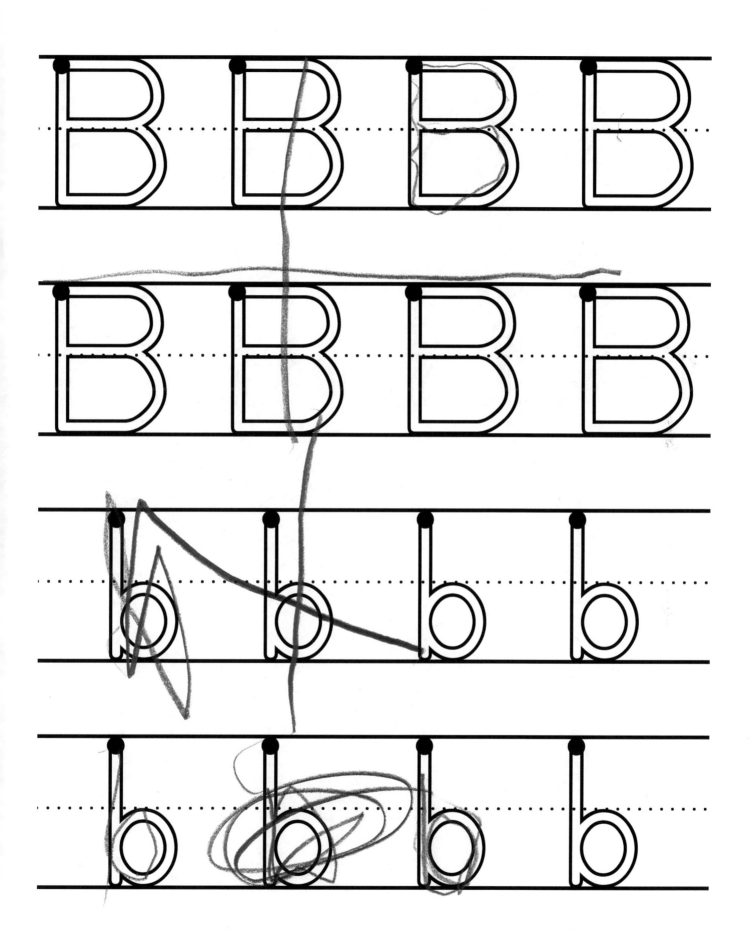

B B B B

B B B B

b b b b

b b b b

B B
b

Cupcake

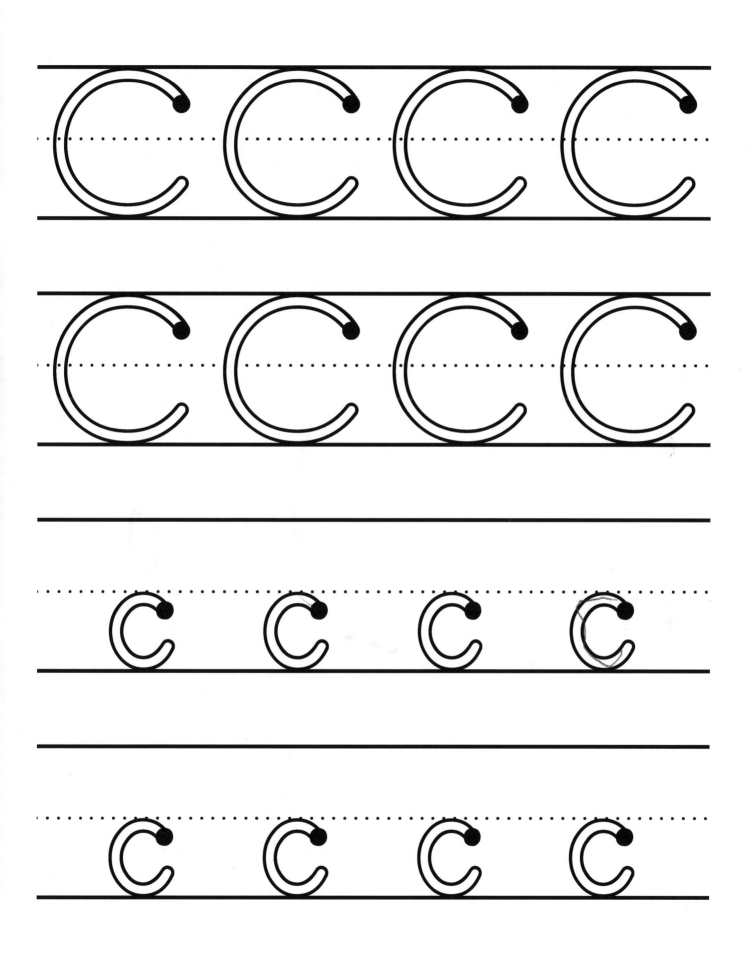

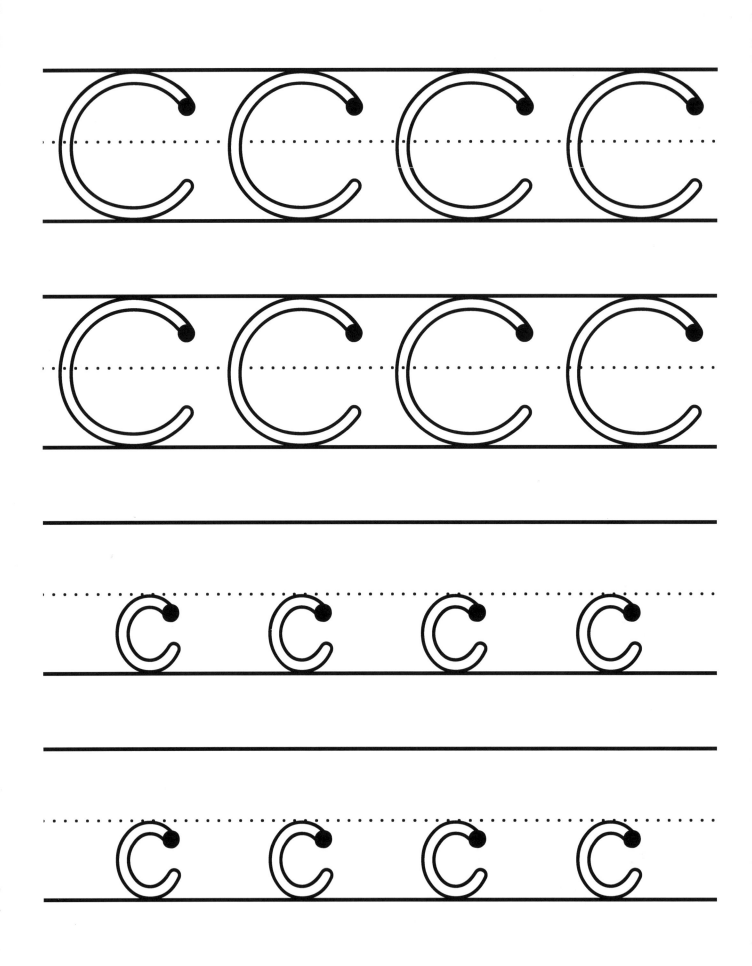

C

C

Dinosaur

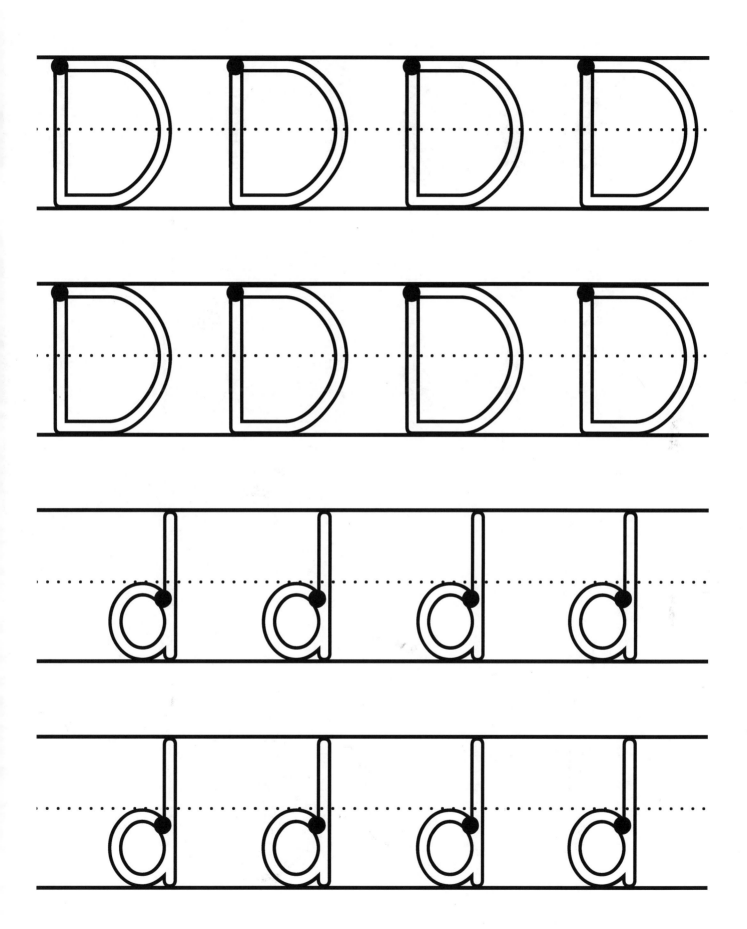

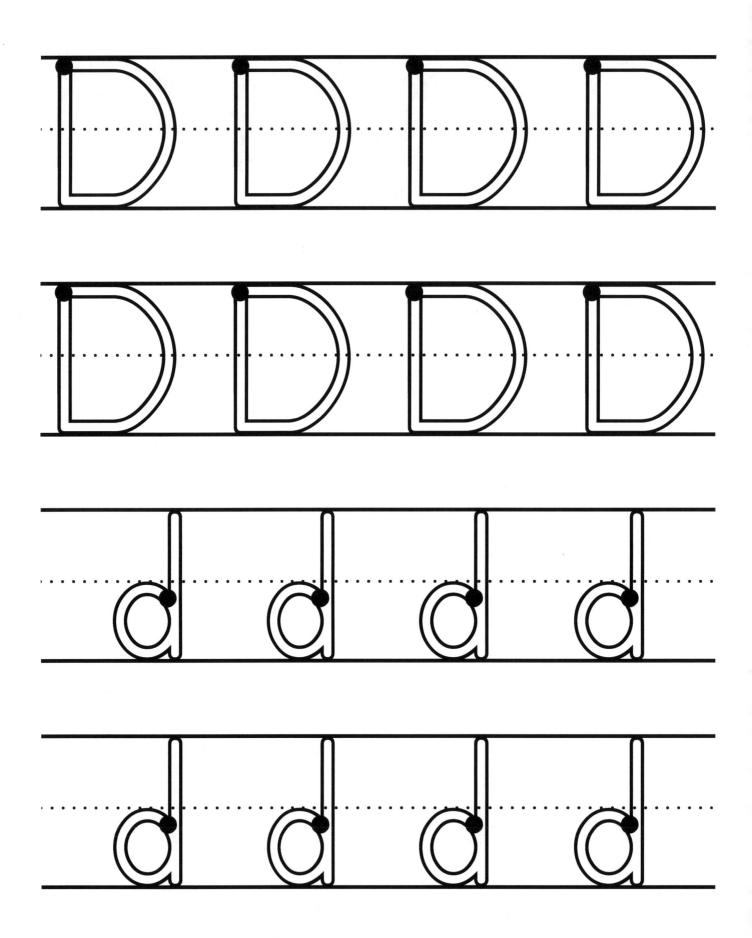

D

d

Elephant

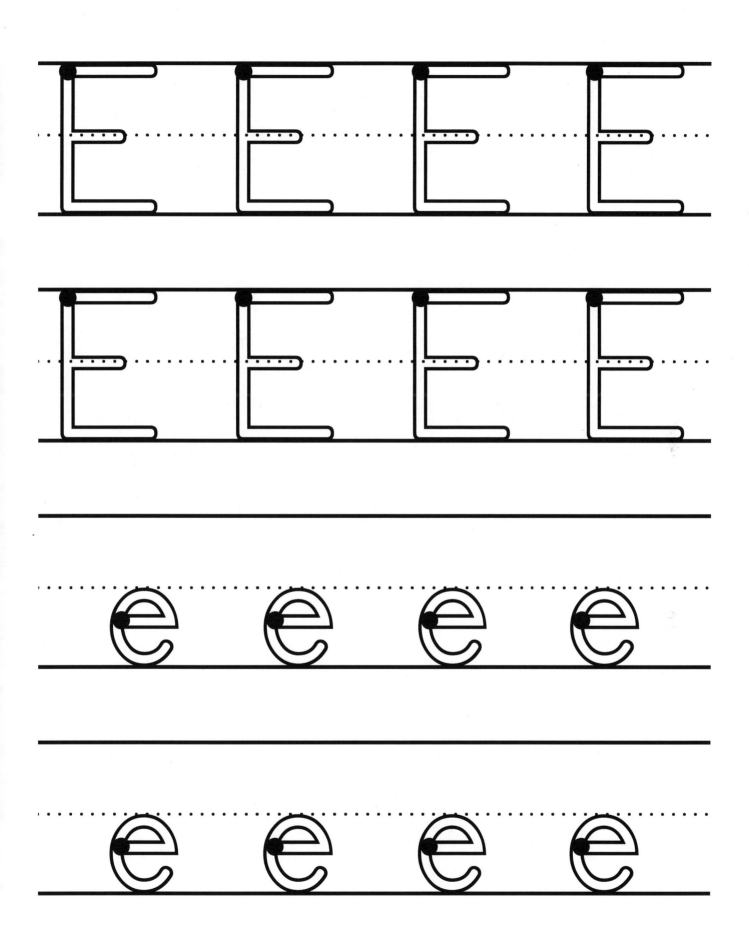

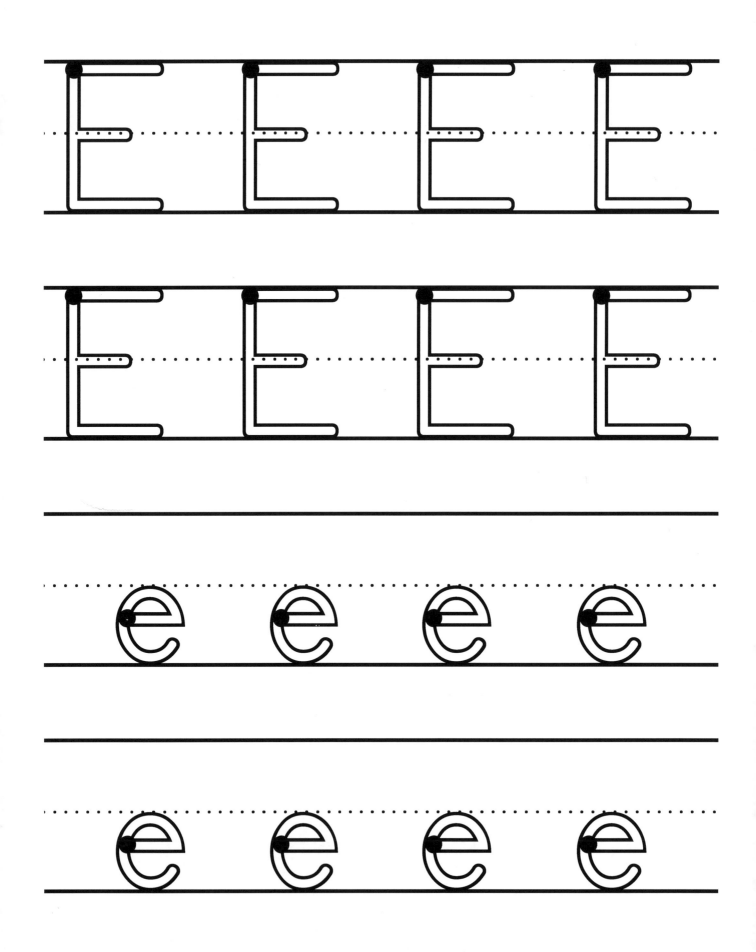

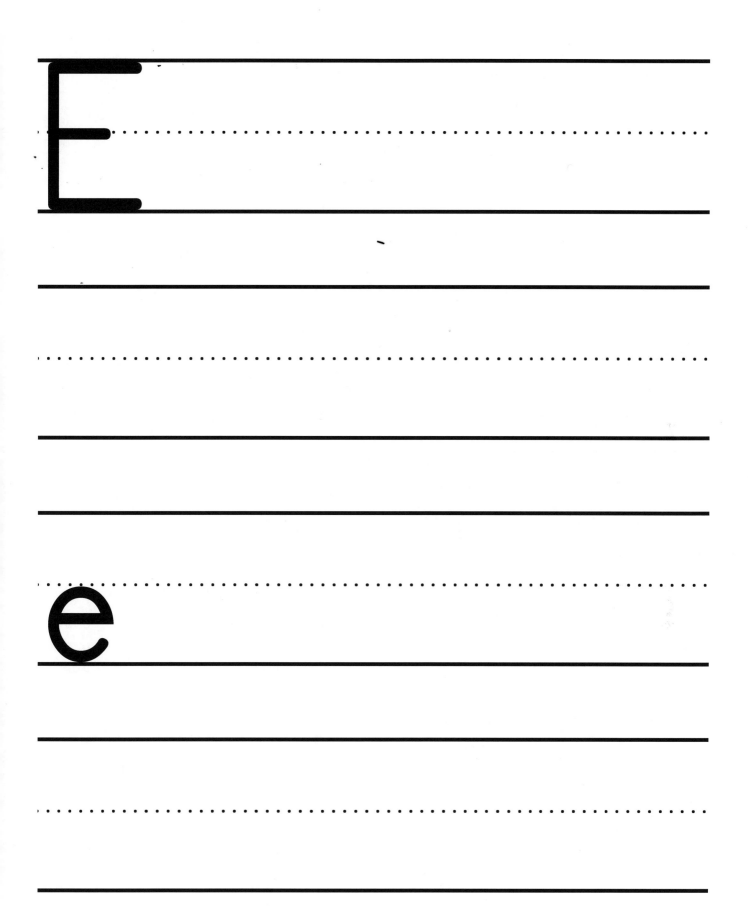

Fish

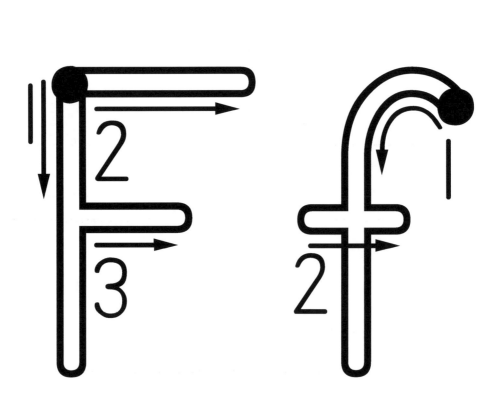

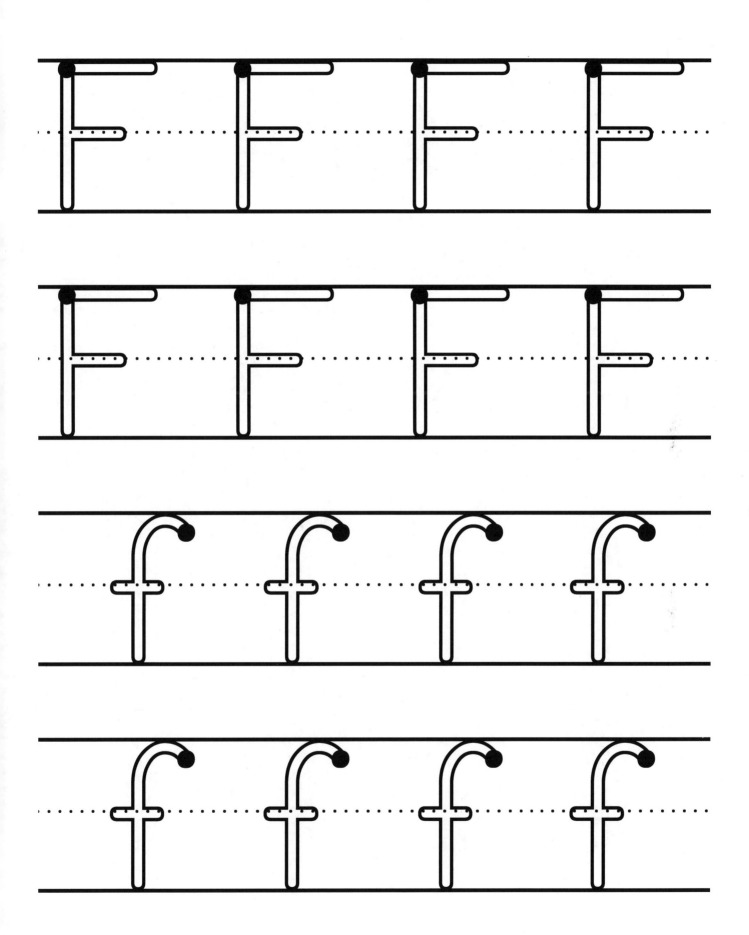

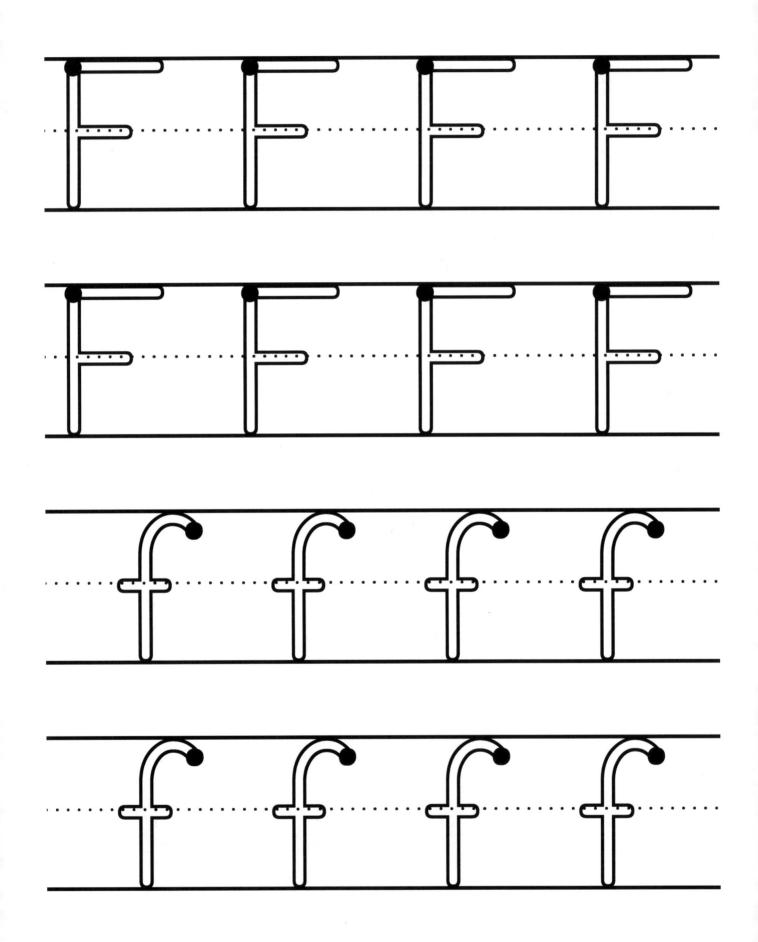

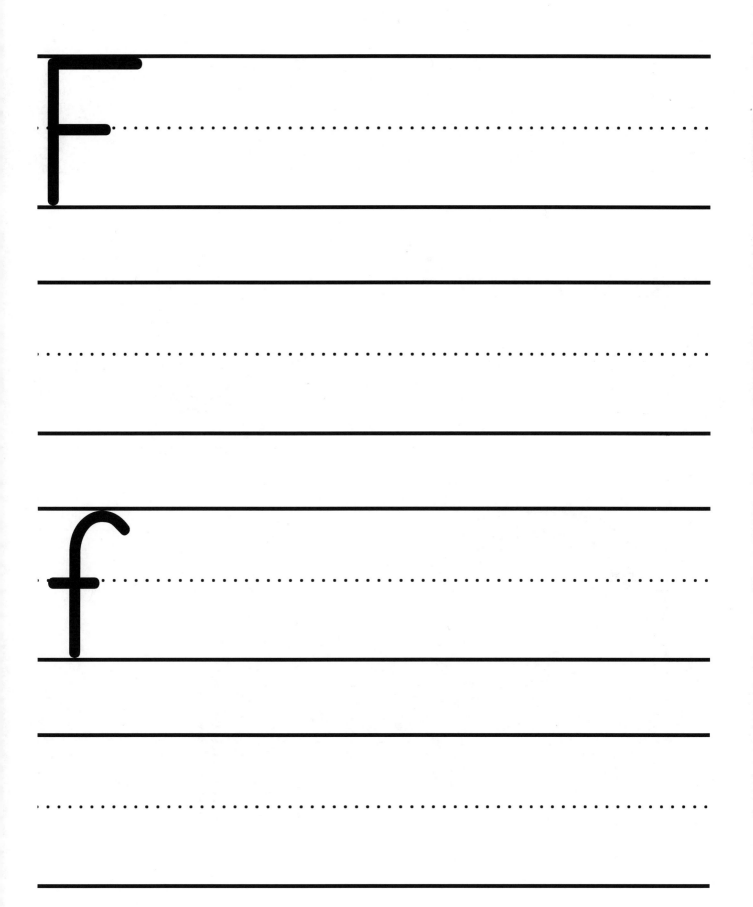

Giraffe

G G G G

G G G G

g g g g

g g g g

G G G G

G G G G

g g g g

g g g g

G

g

Hippo

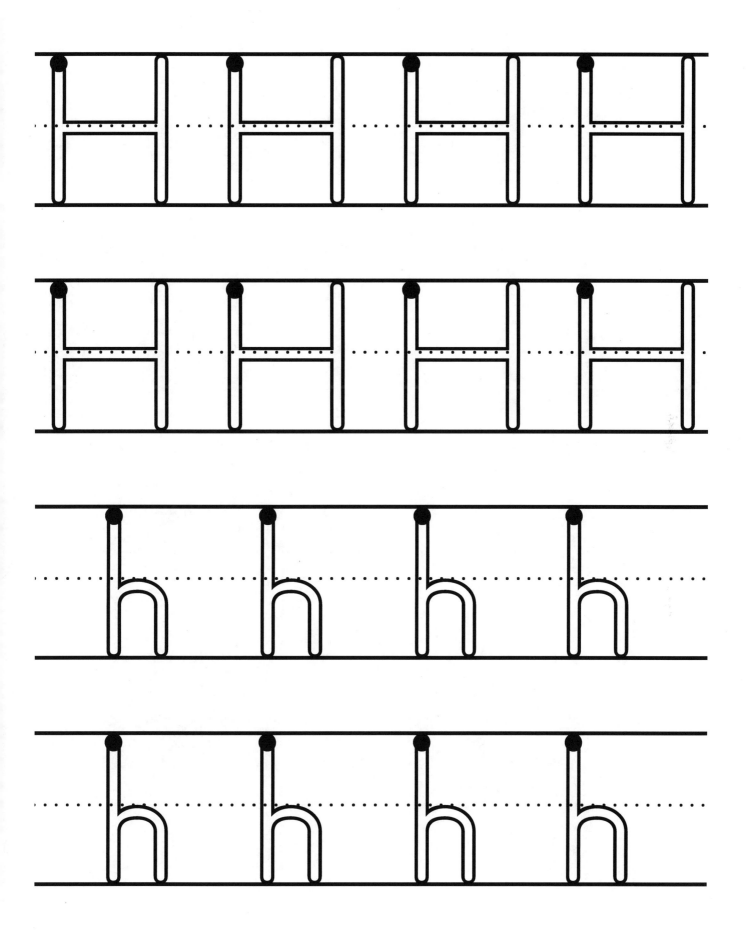

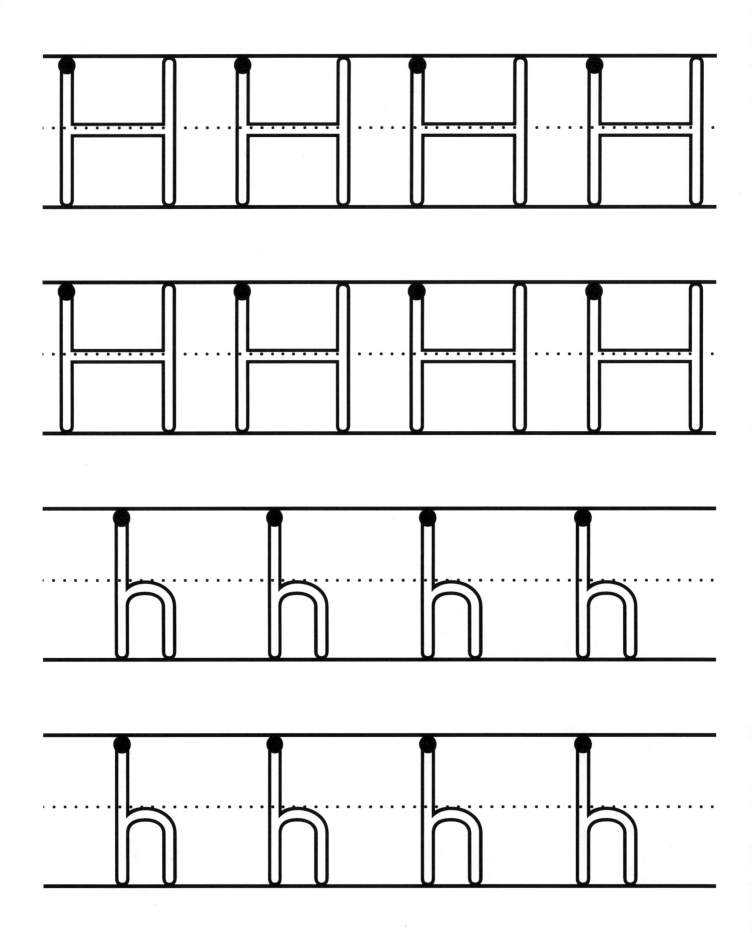

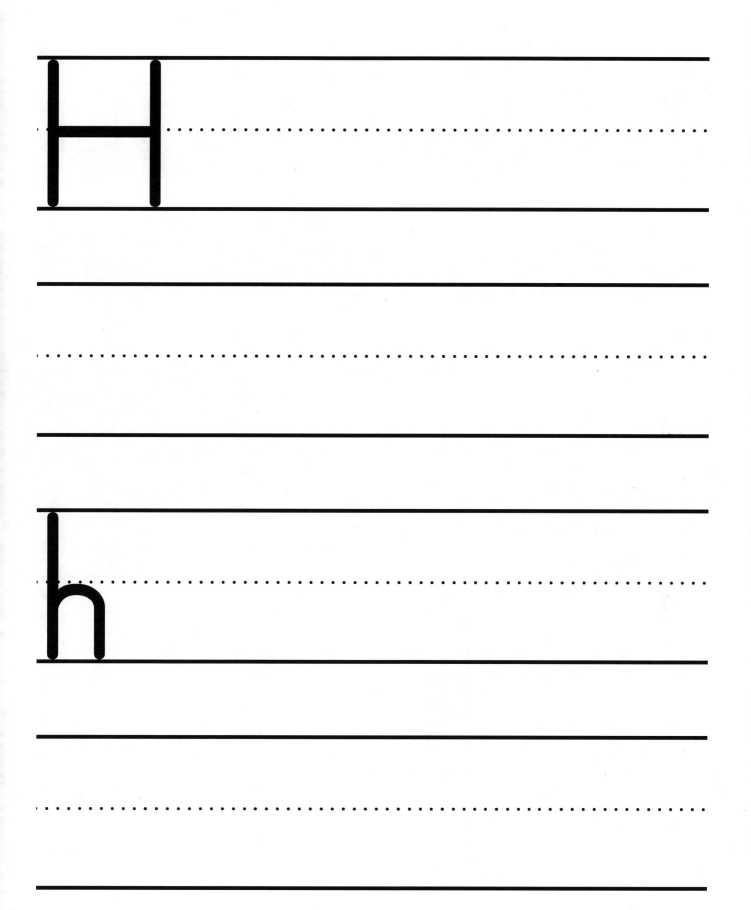

Icecream

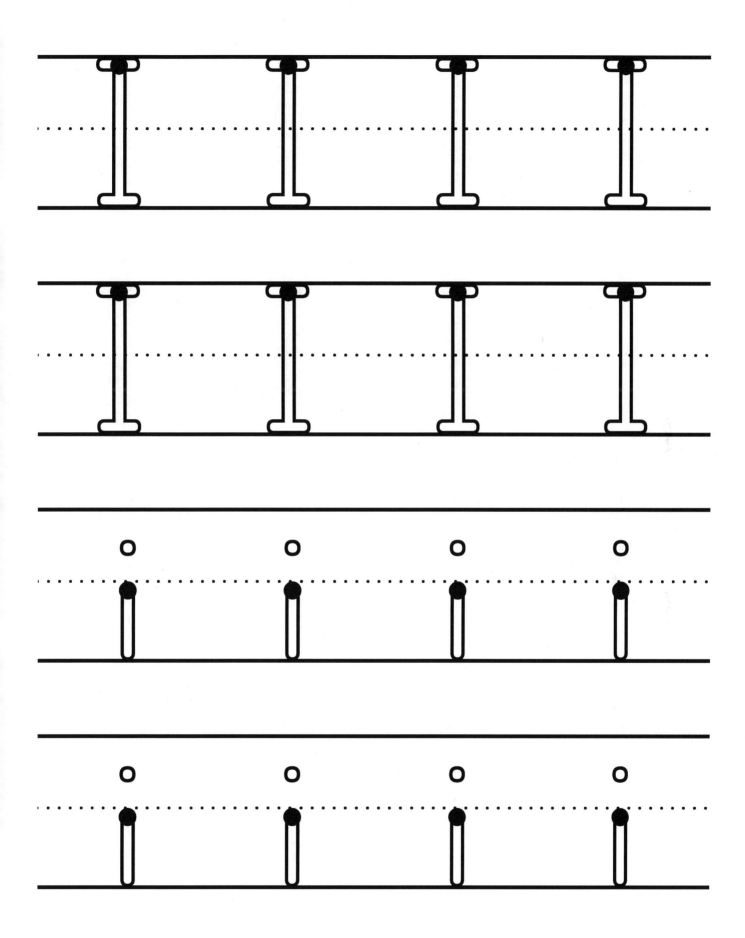

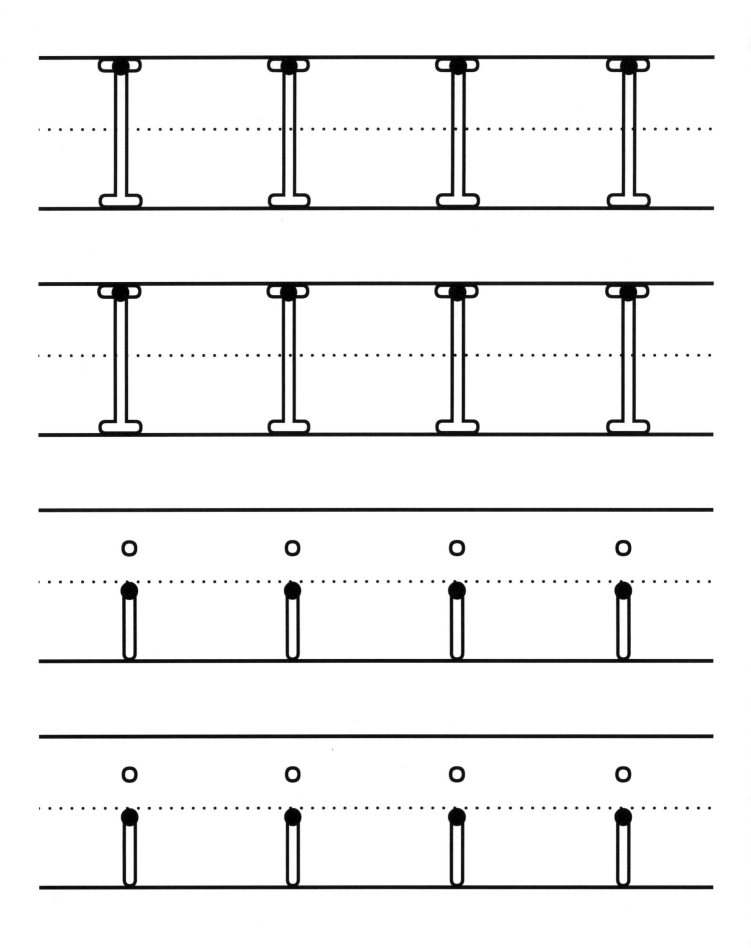

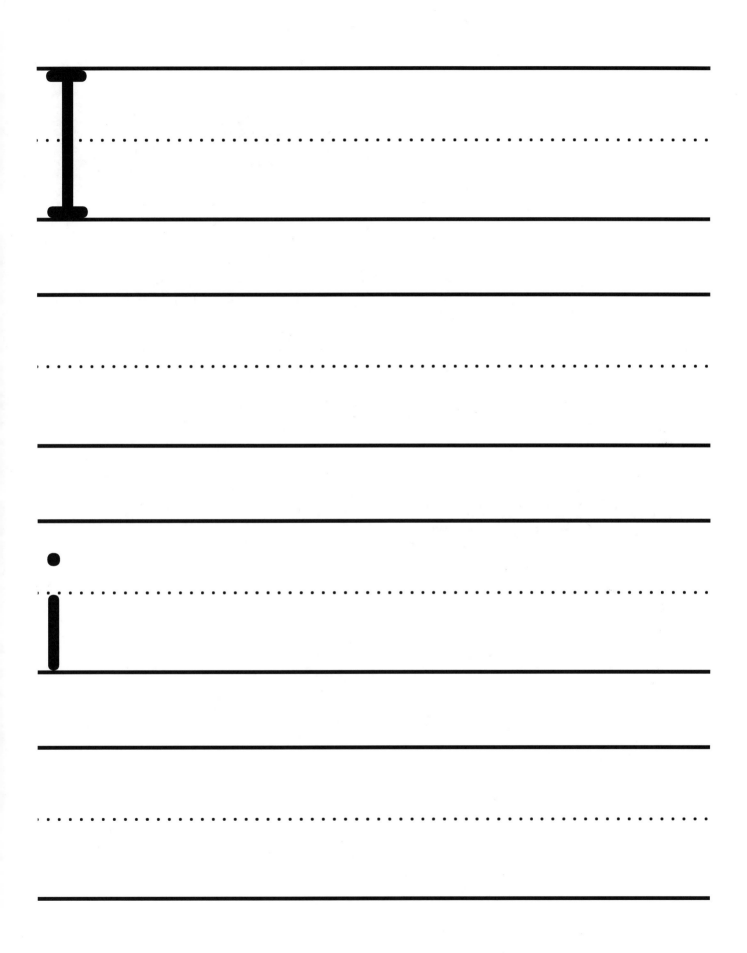

Jellyfish

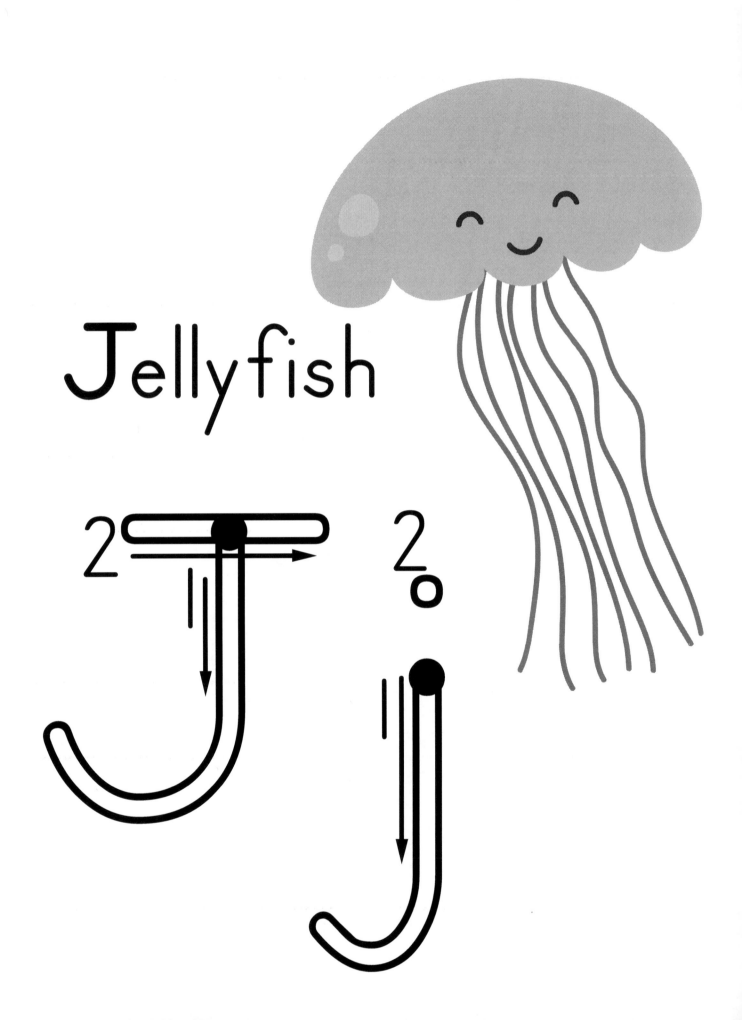

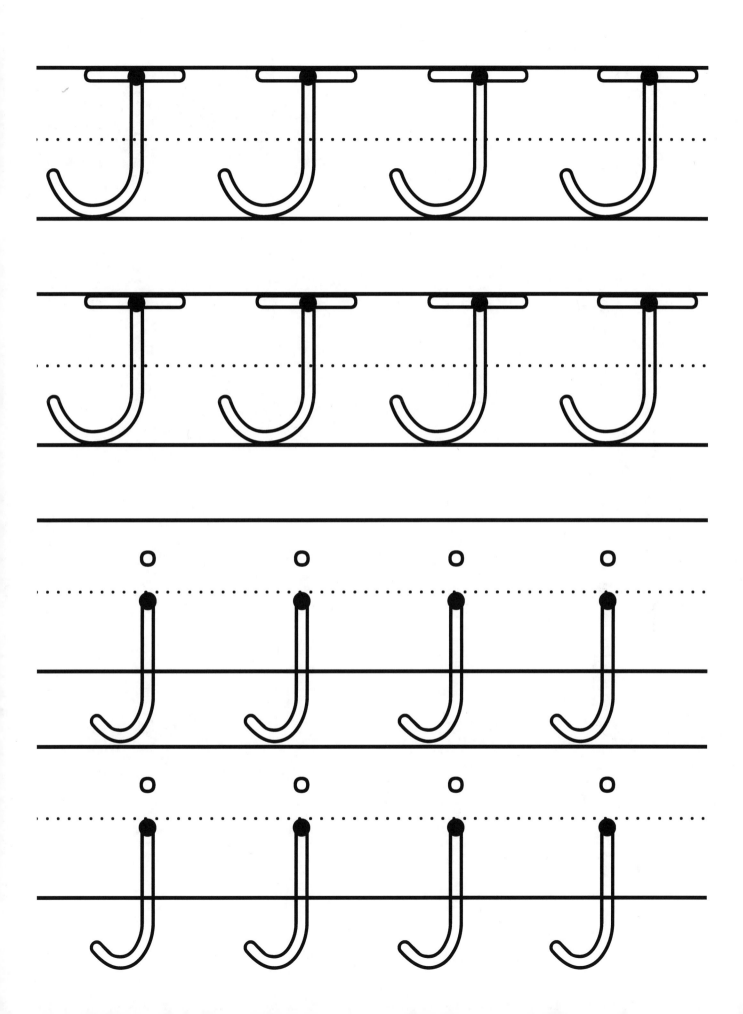

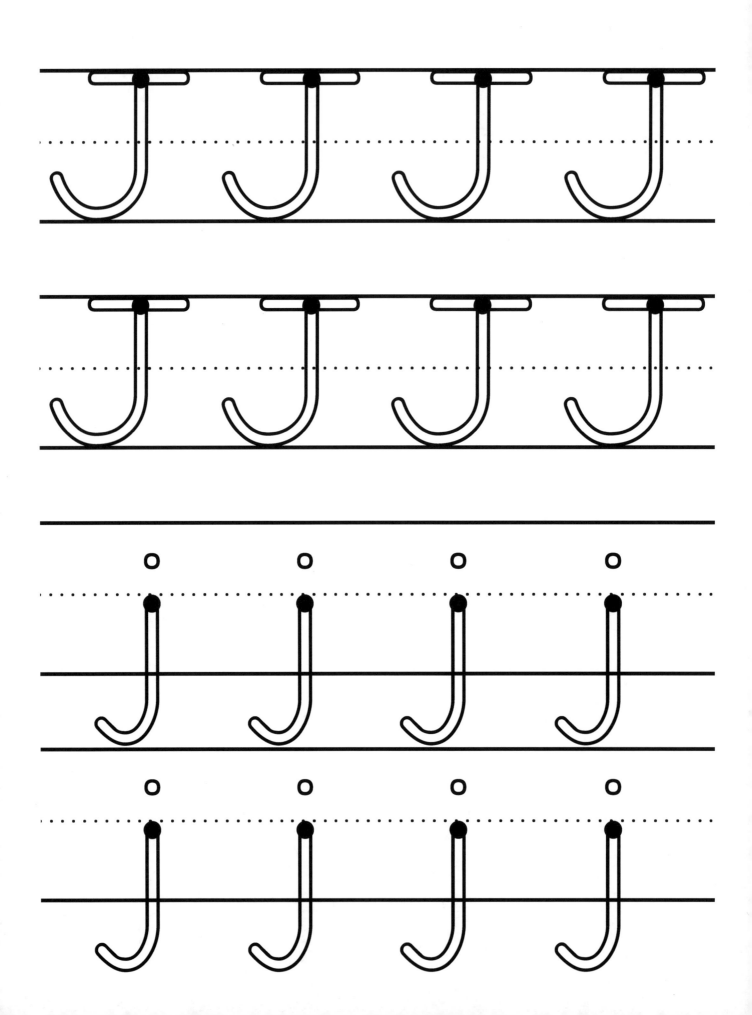

J

j

Kite

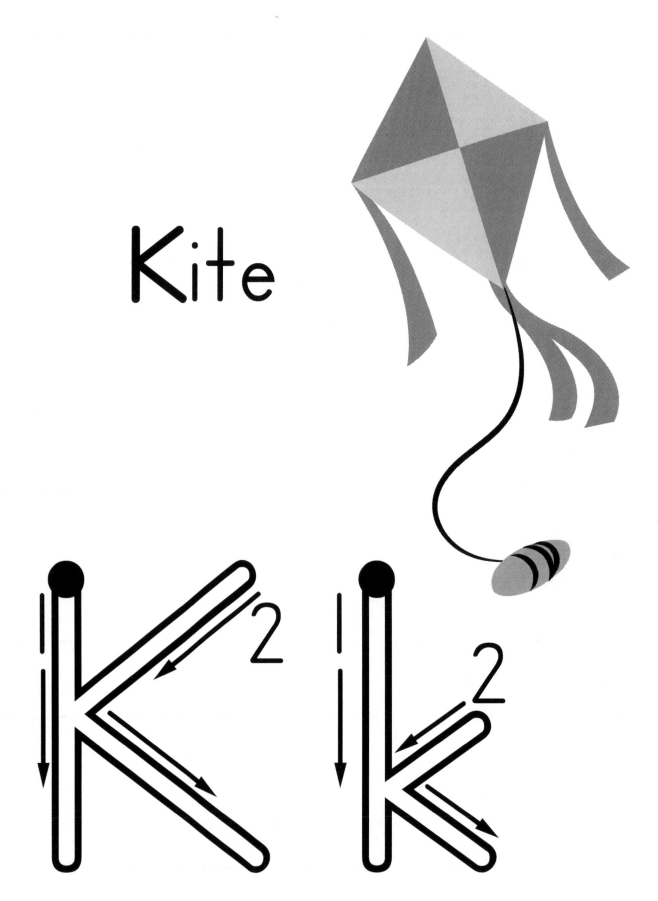

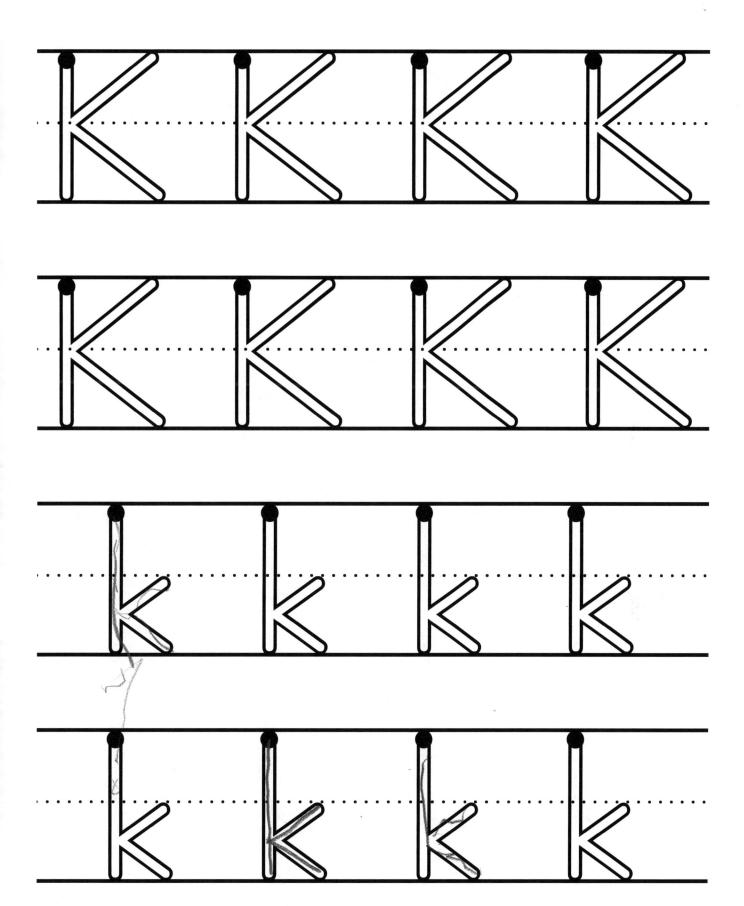

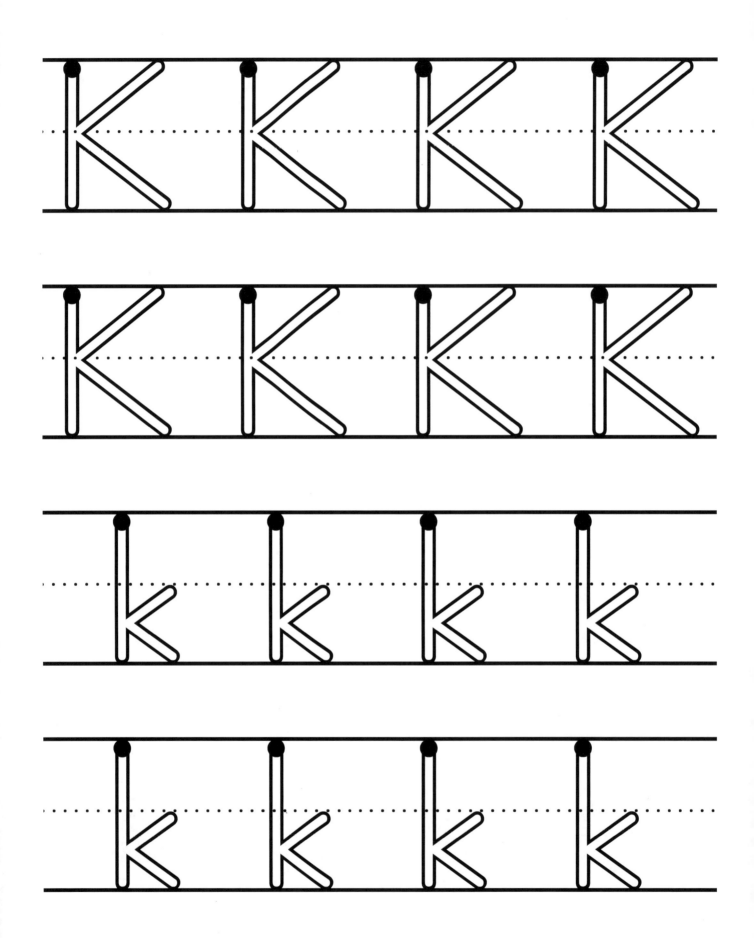

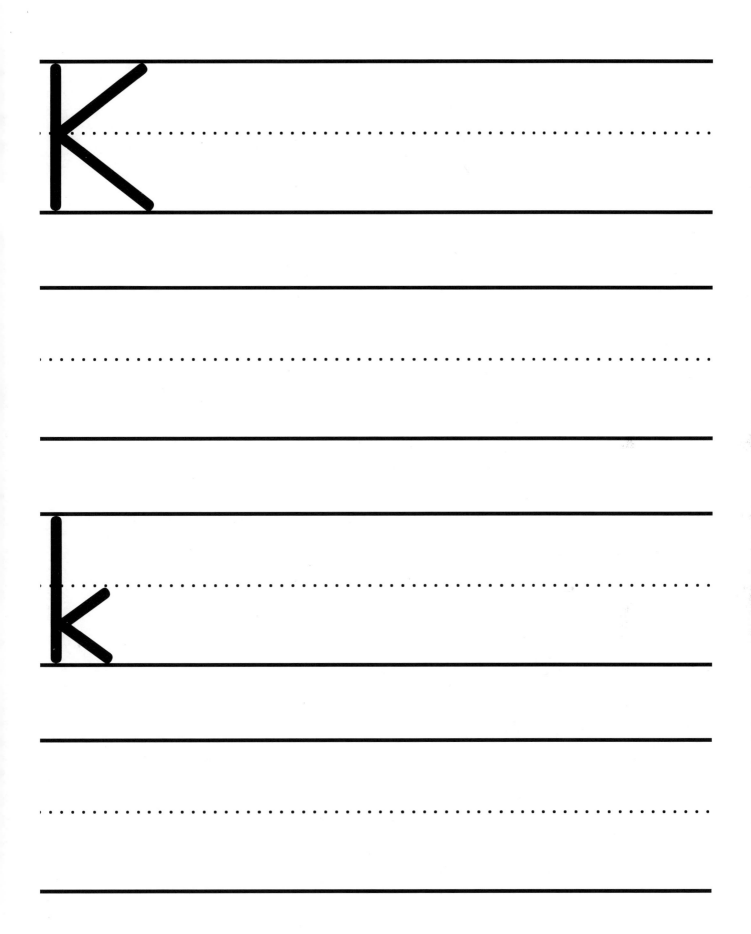

Lion

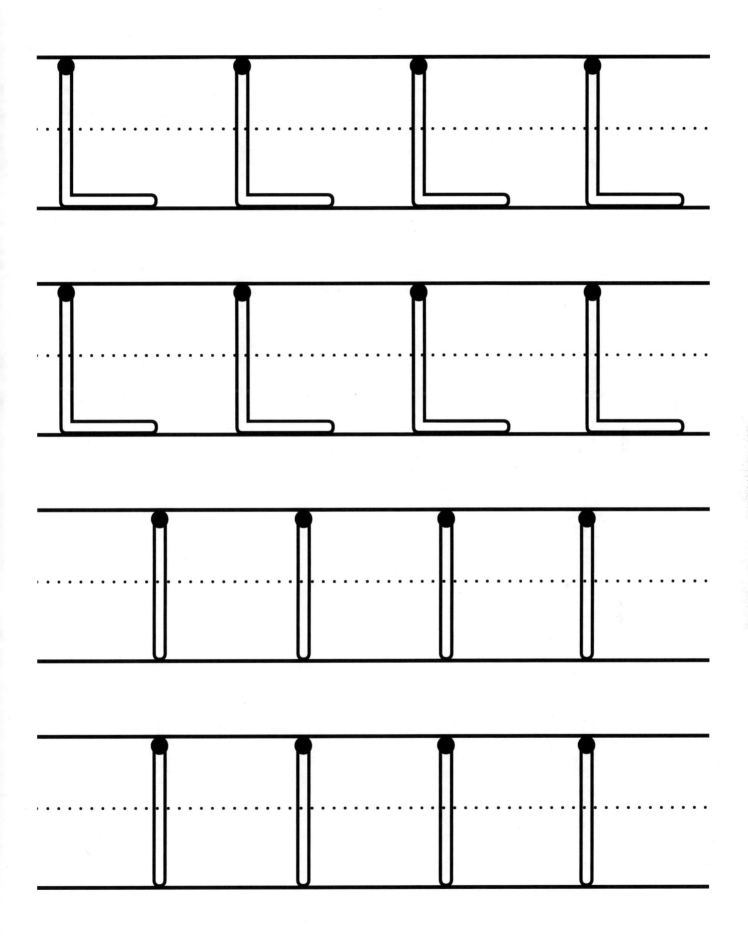

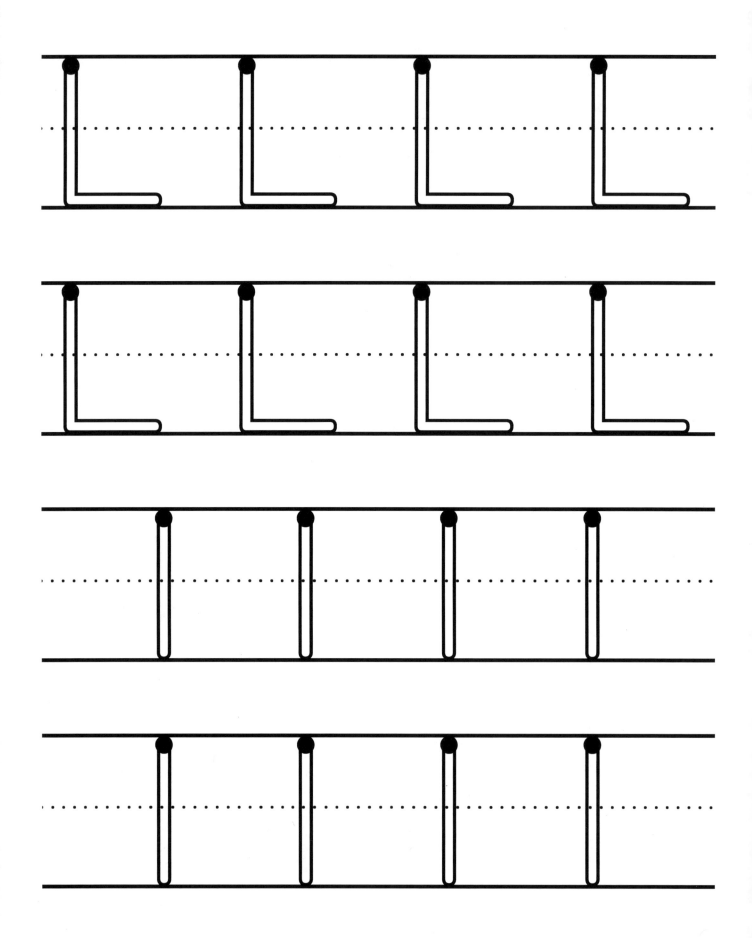

Monkey

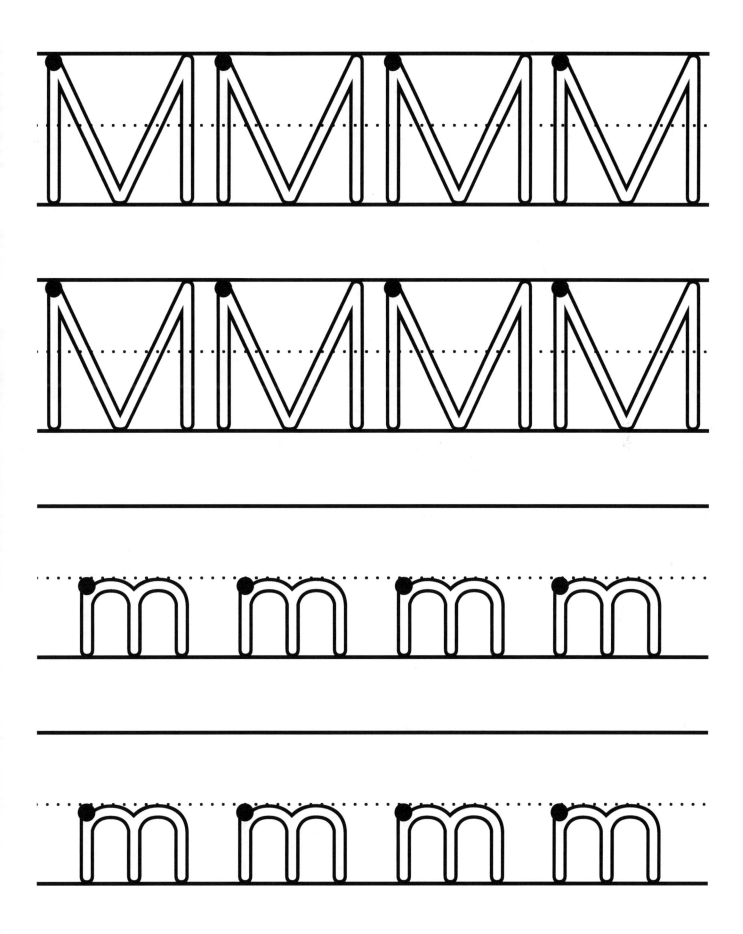

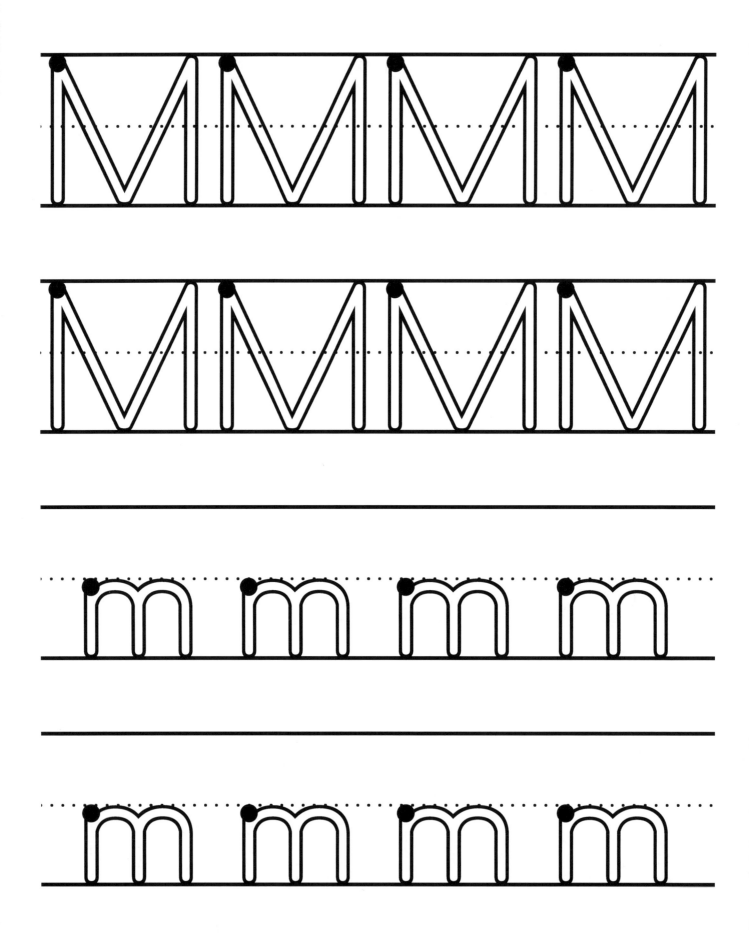

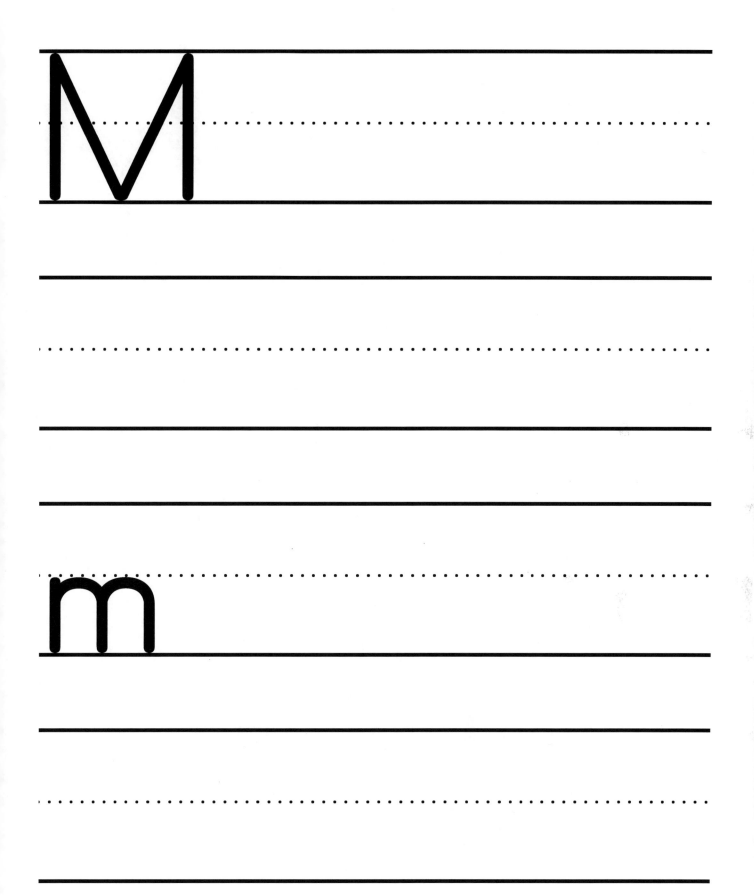

Ninja

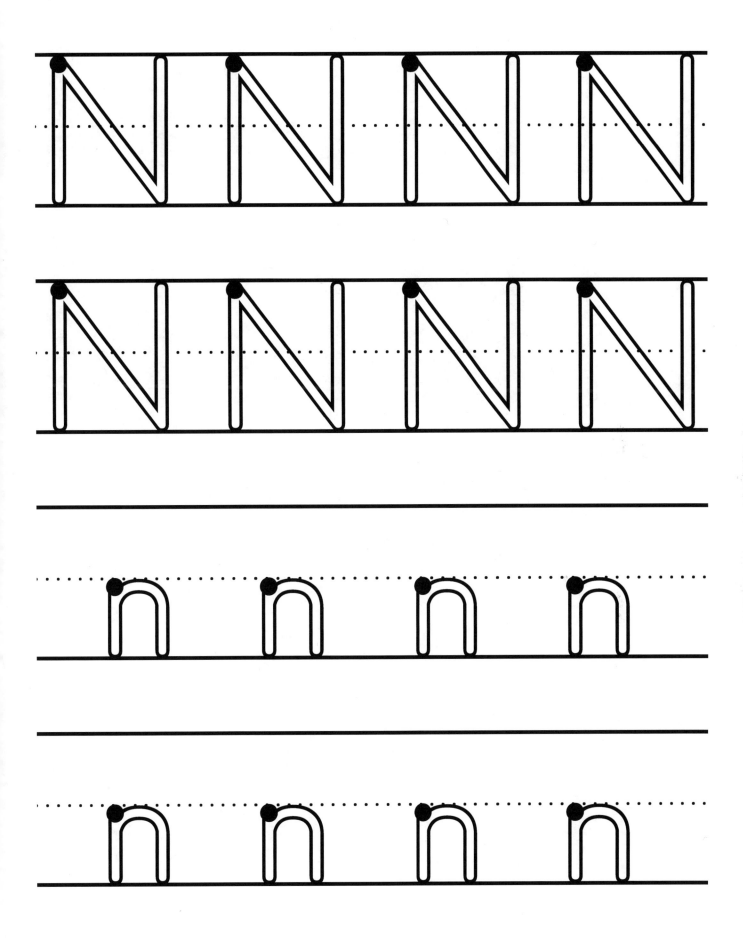

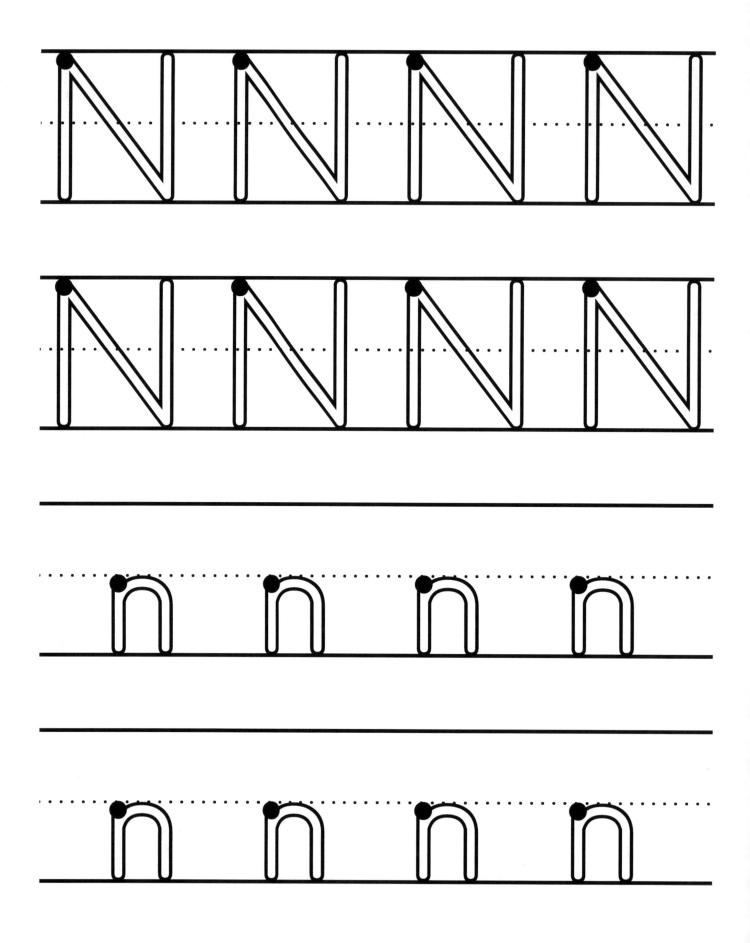

Owl

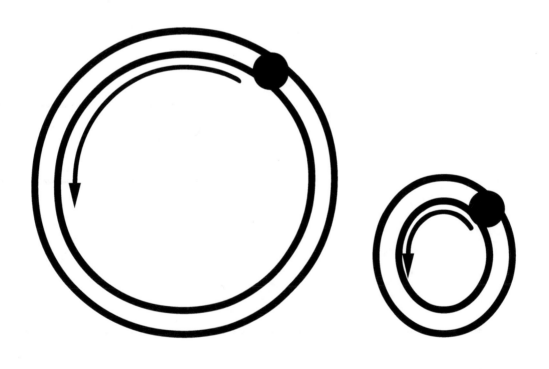

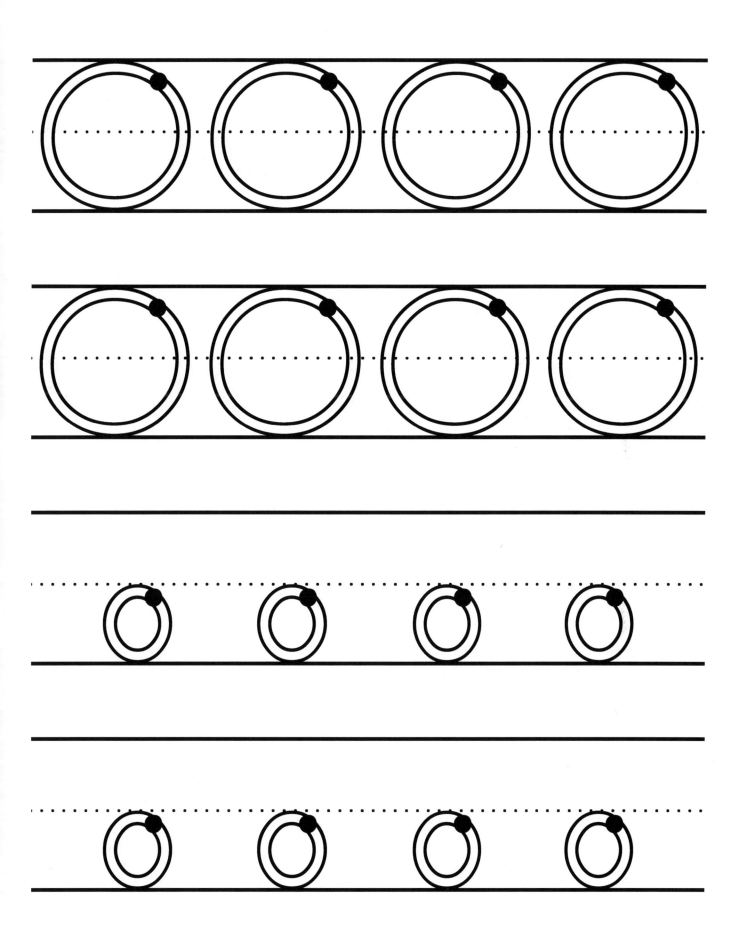

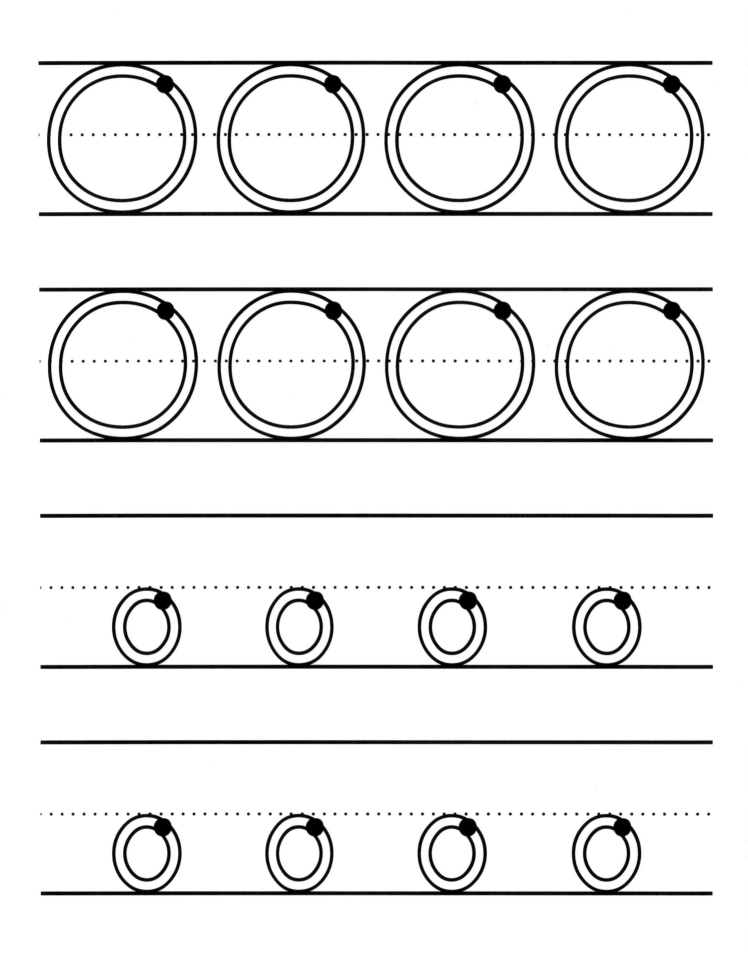

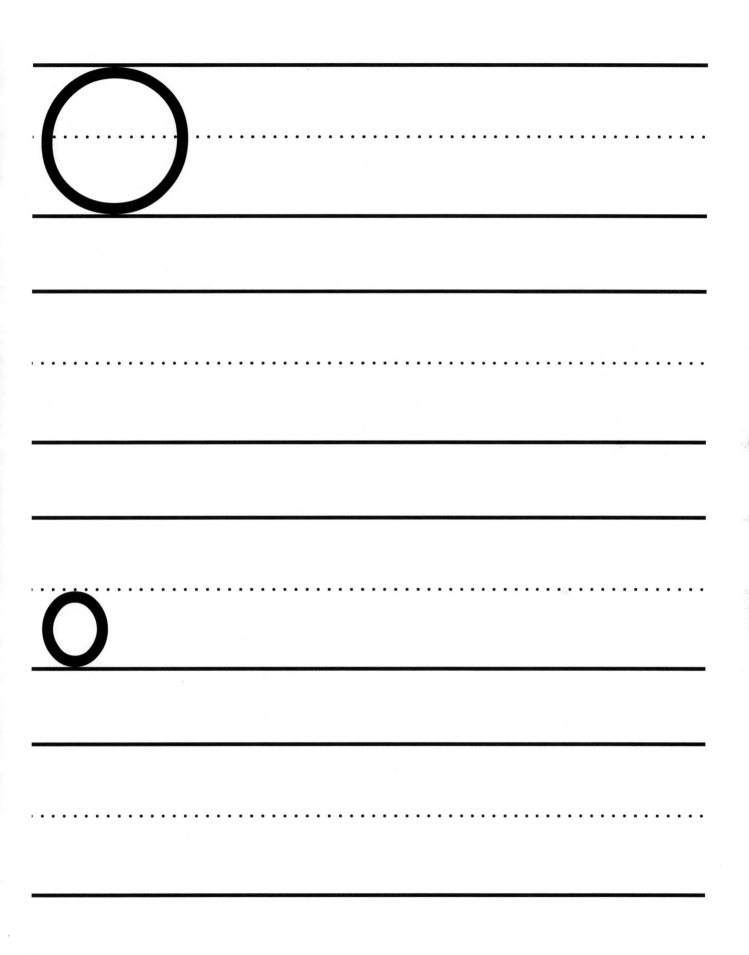

Pineapple

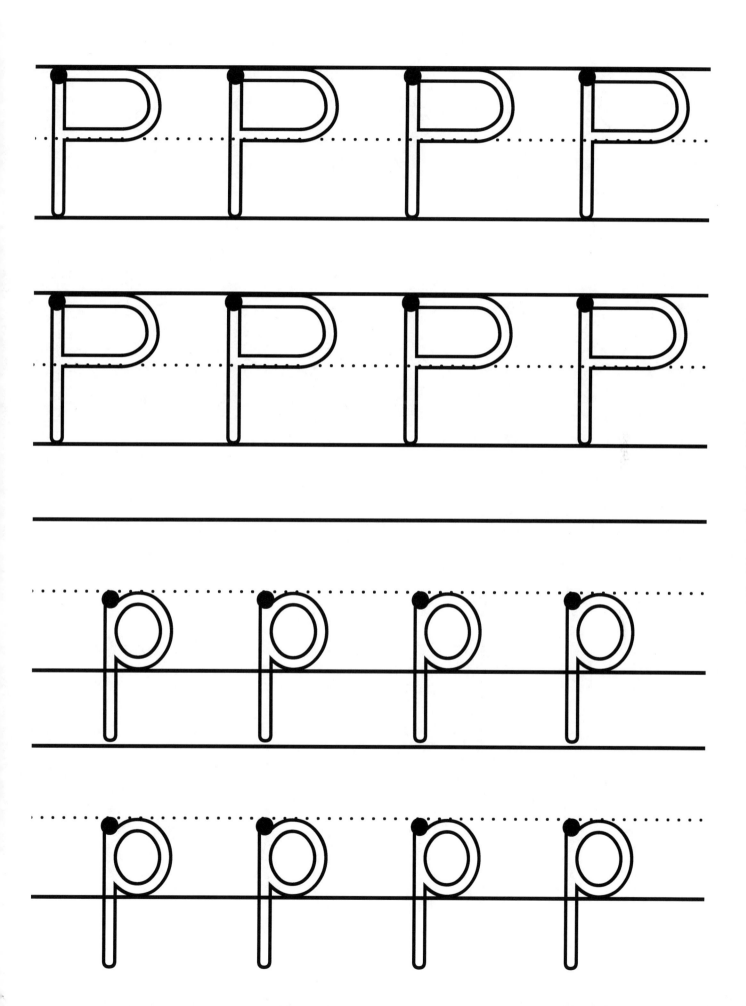

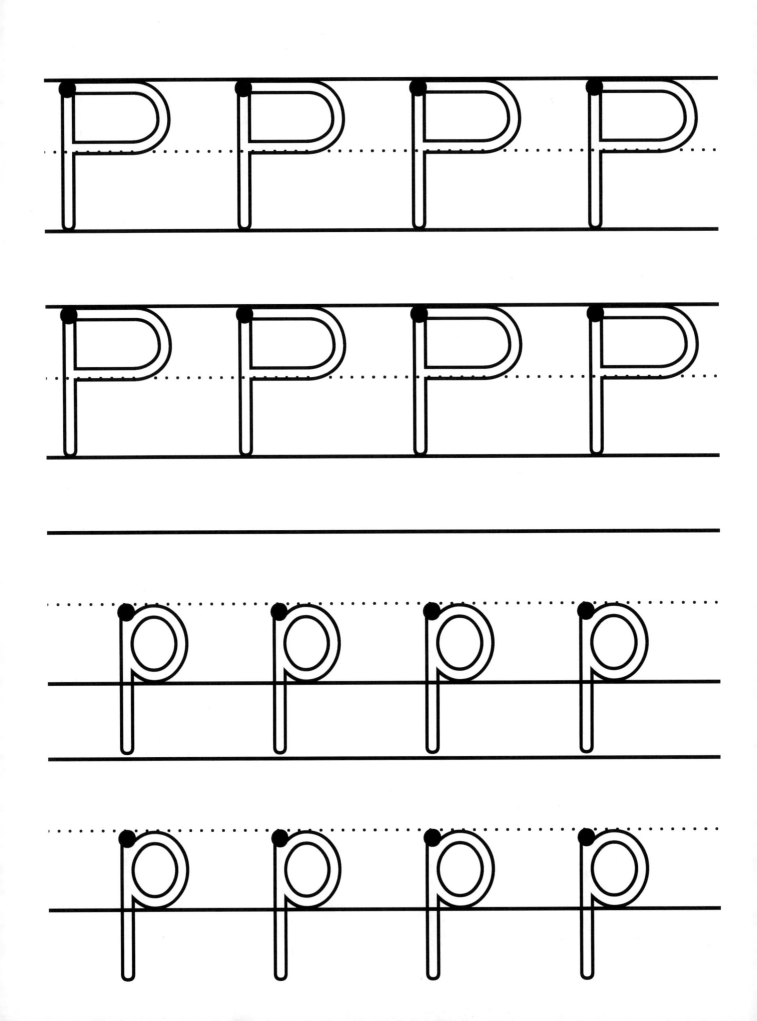

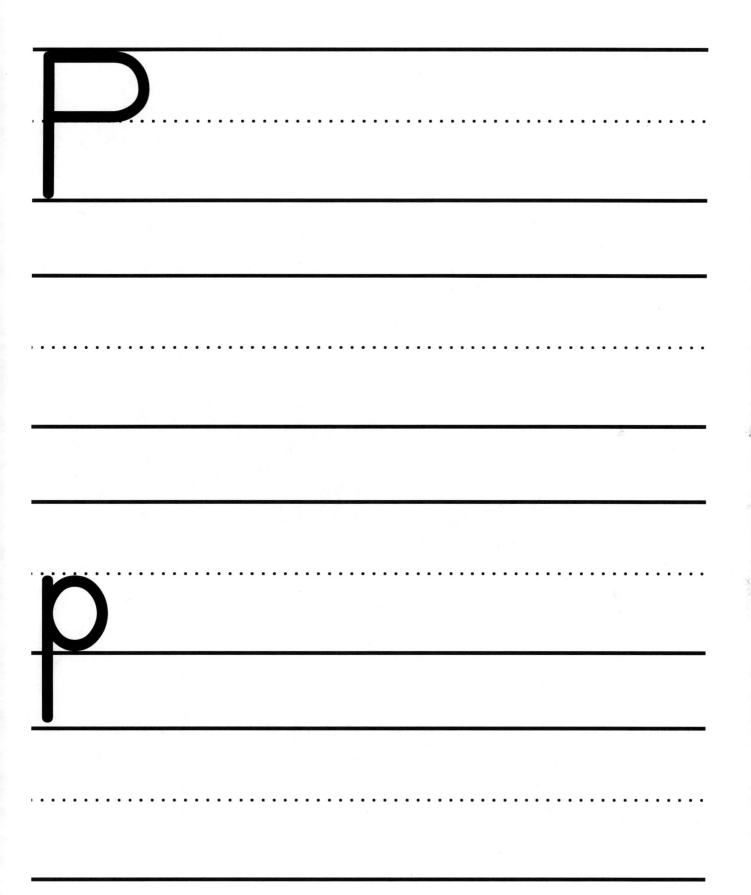

Queen

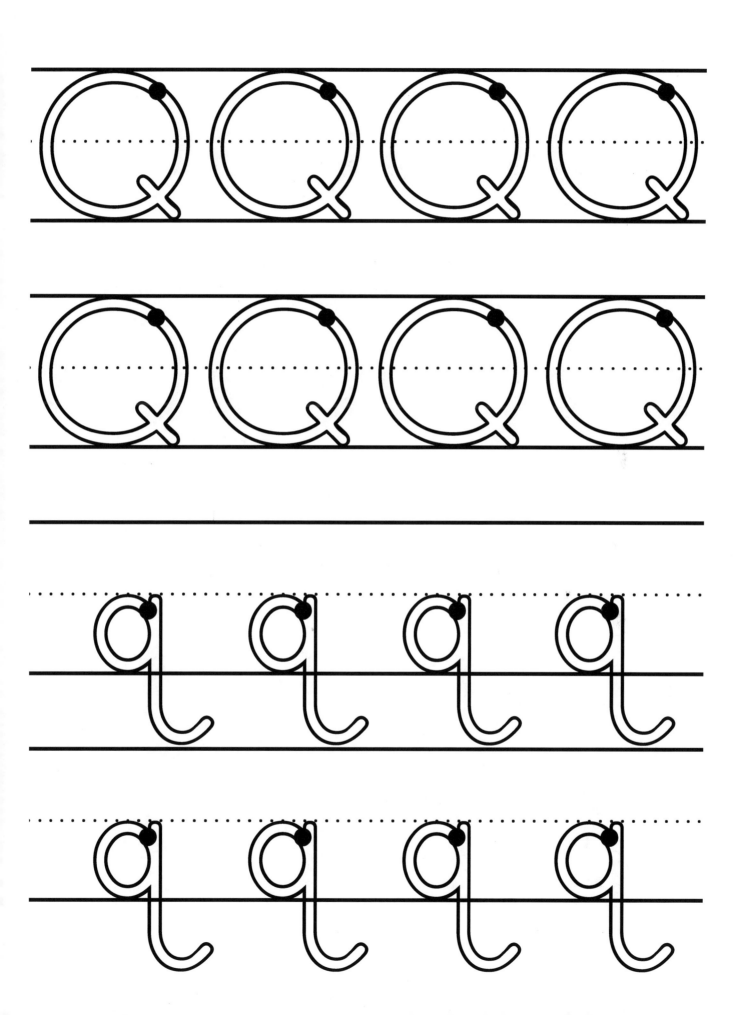

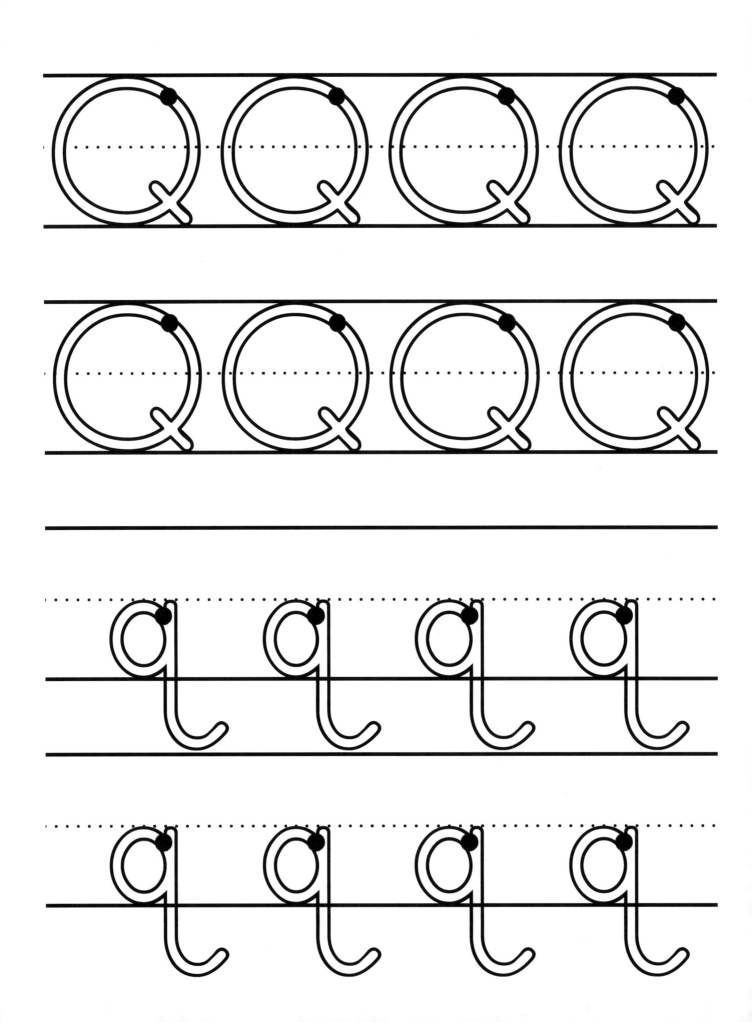

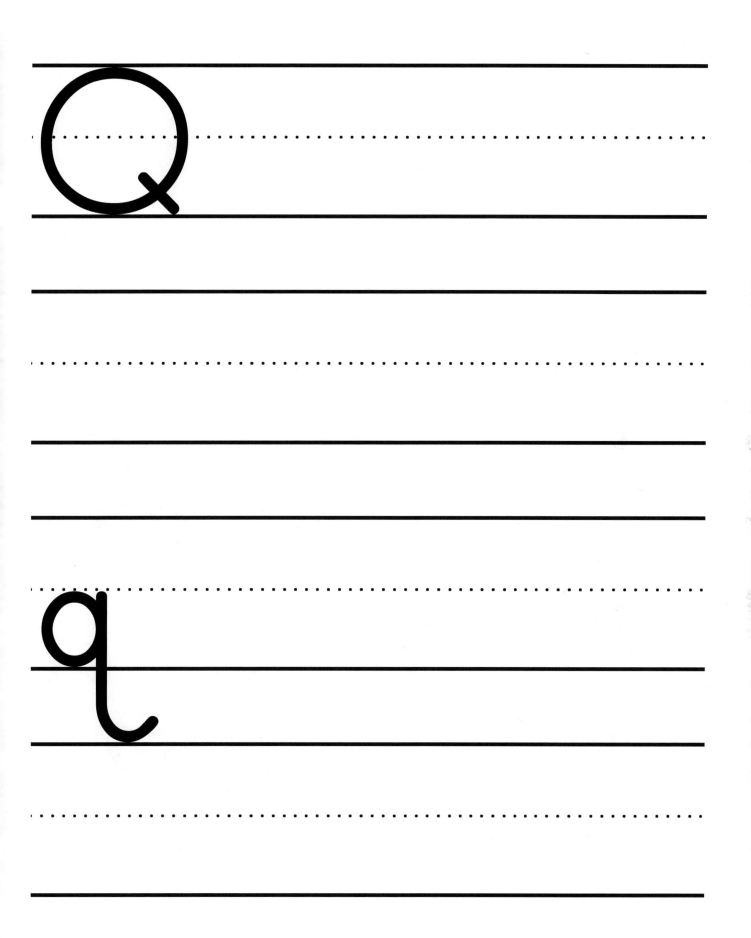

Robot

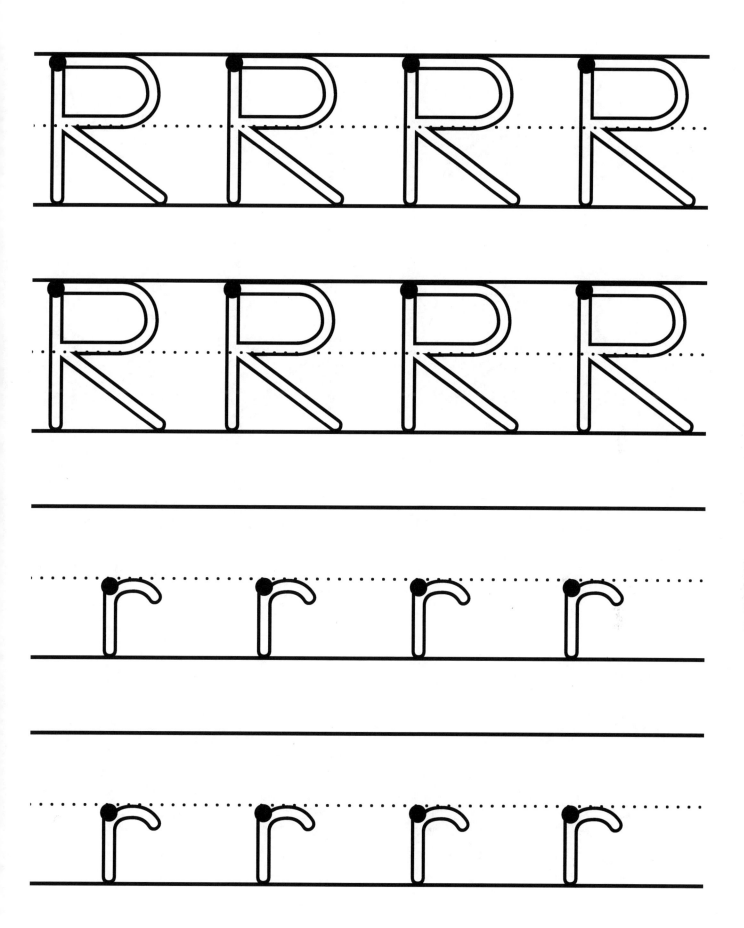

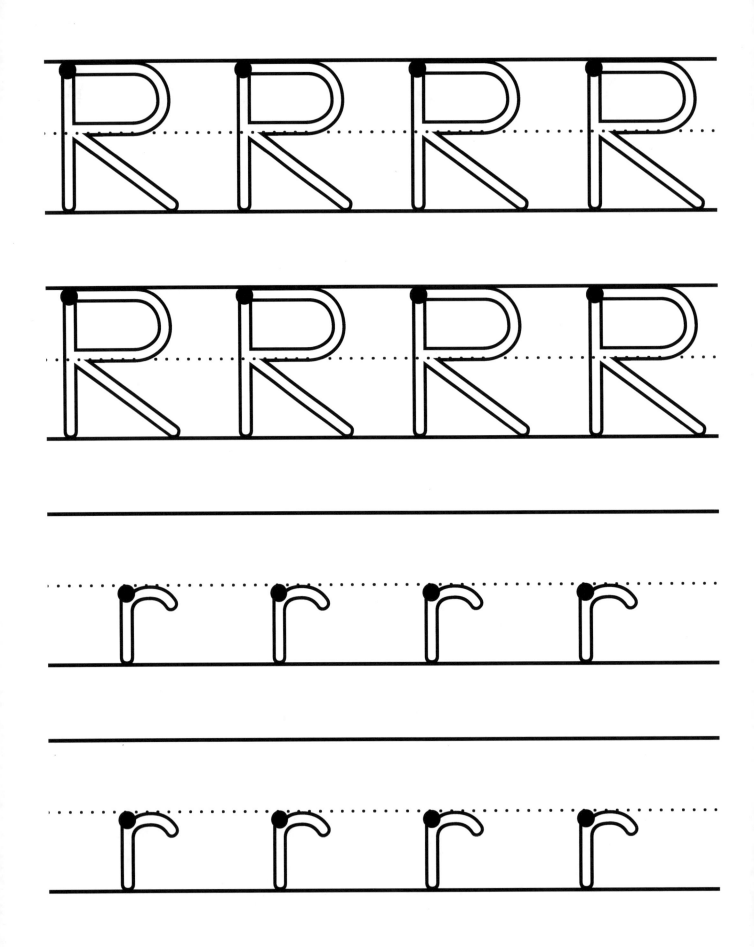

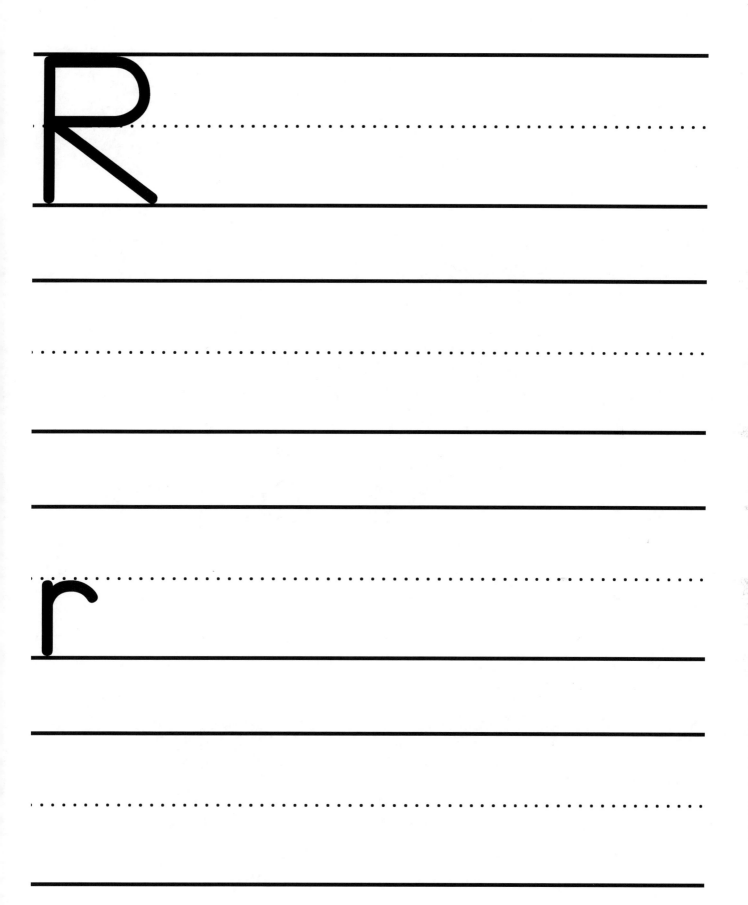

Shark

S s

S S S S

S S S S

s s s s

s s s s

S S S S

S S S S

s s s s

s s s s

S

s

Train

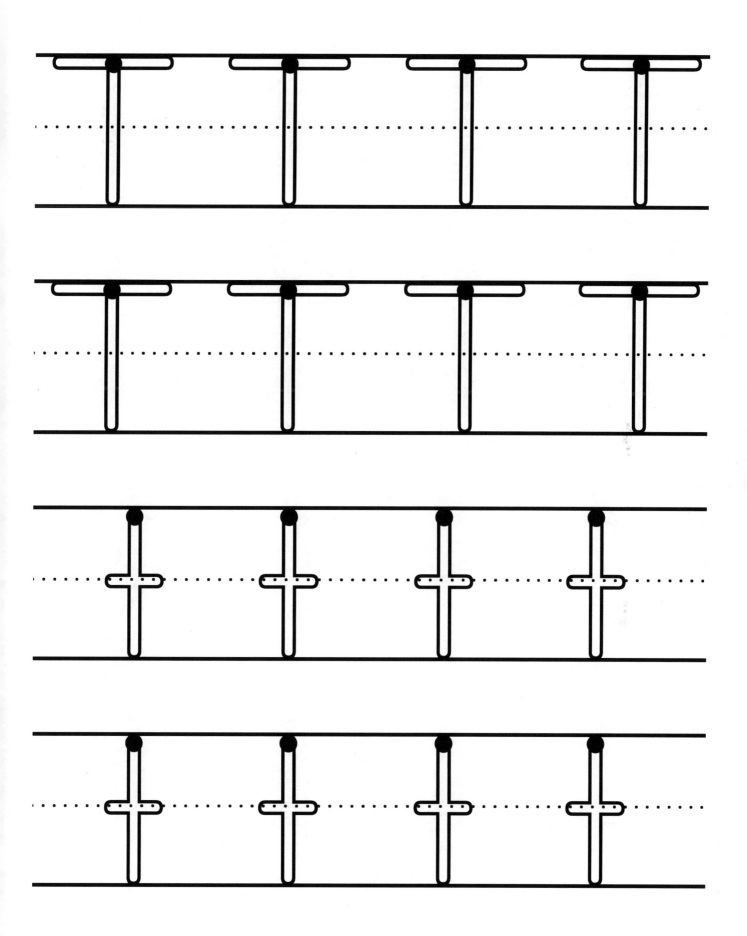

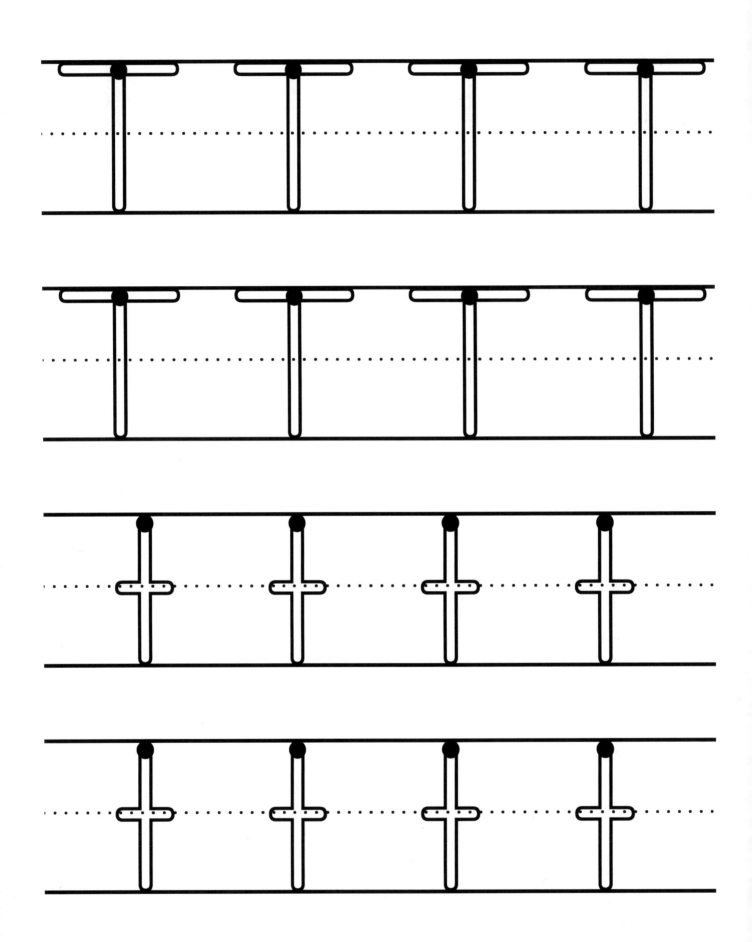

T

t

Unicorn

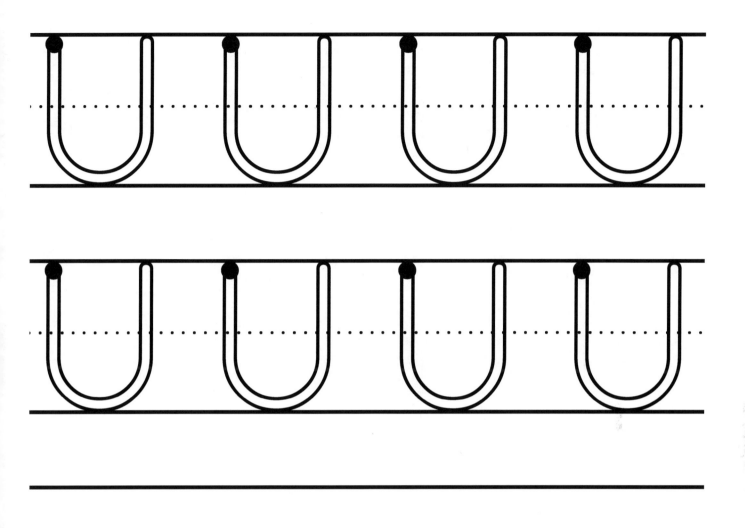

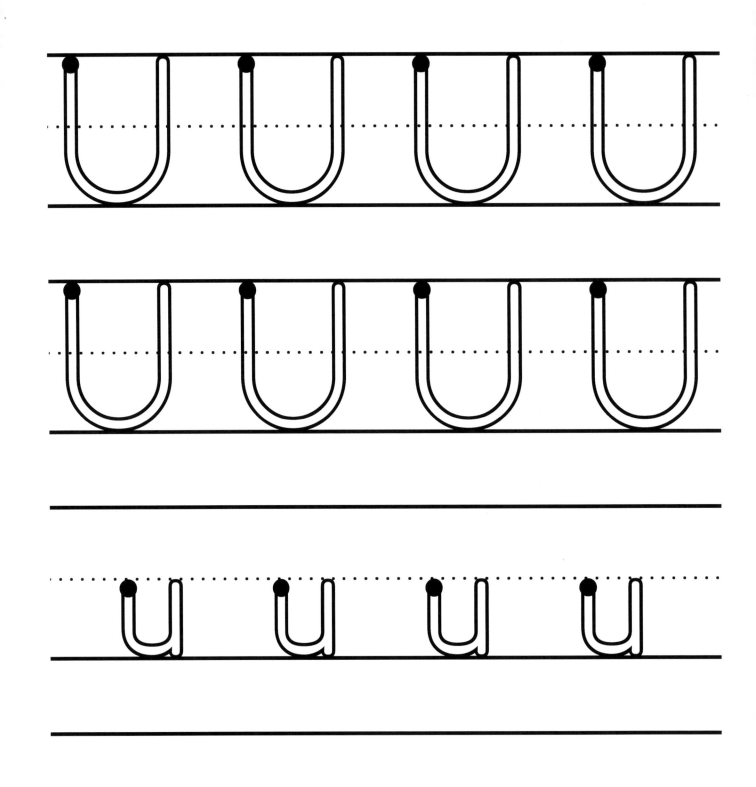

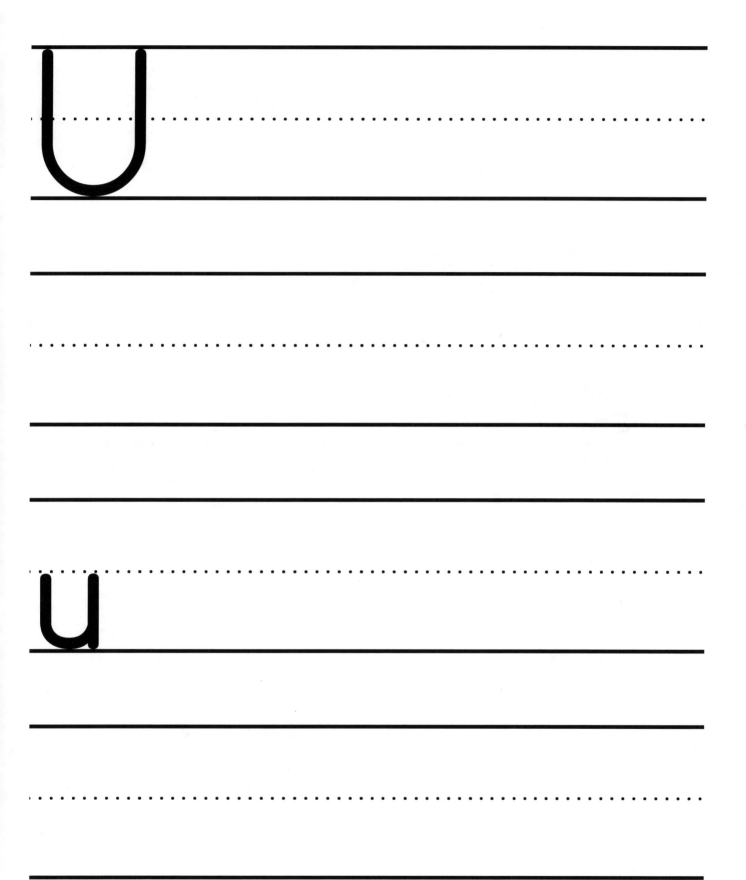

Van

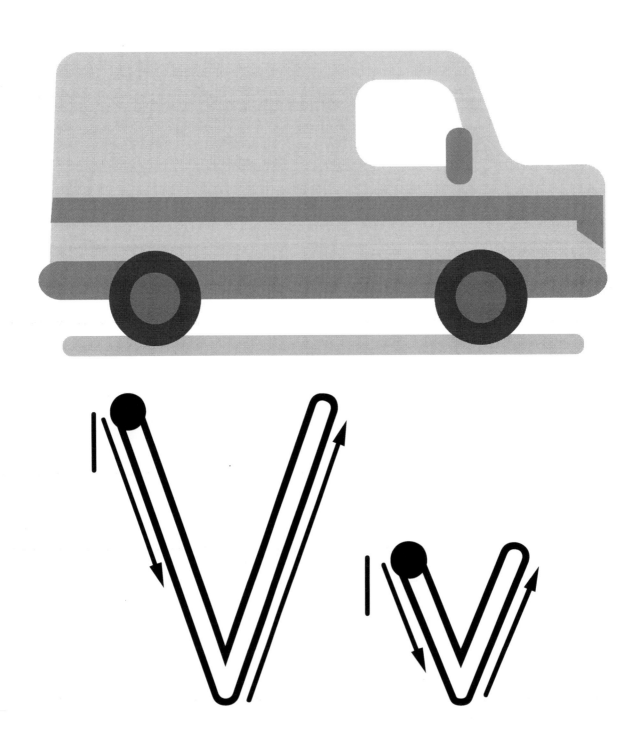

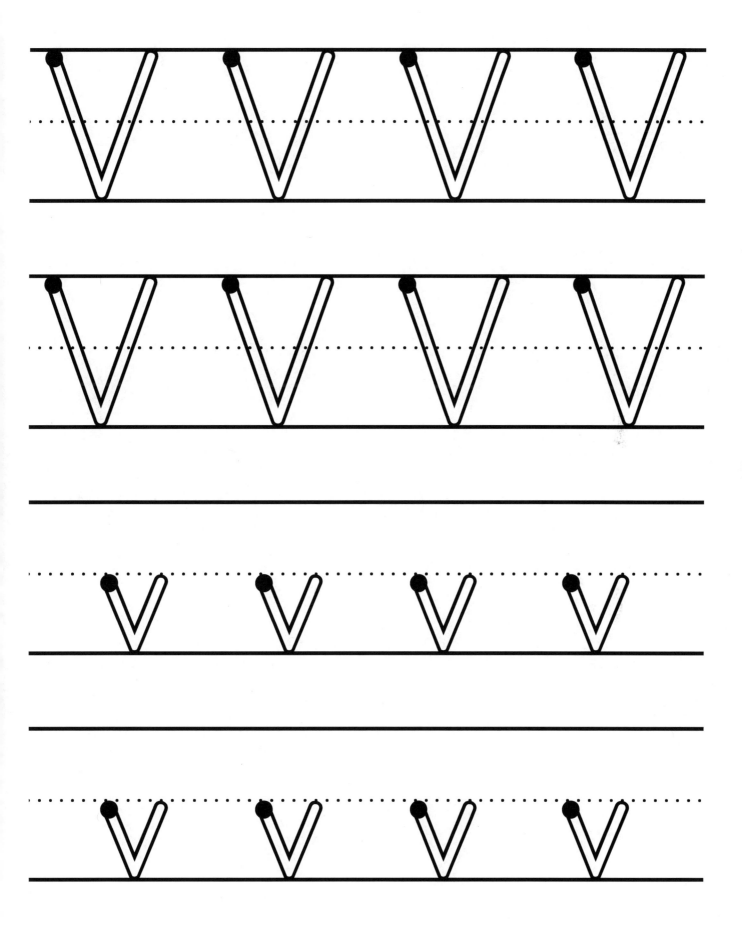

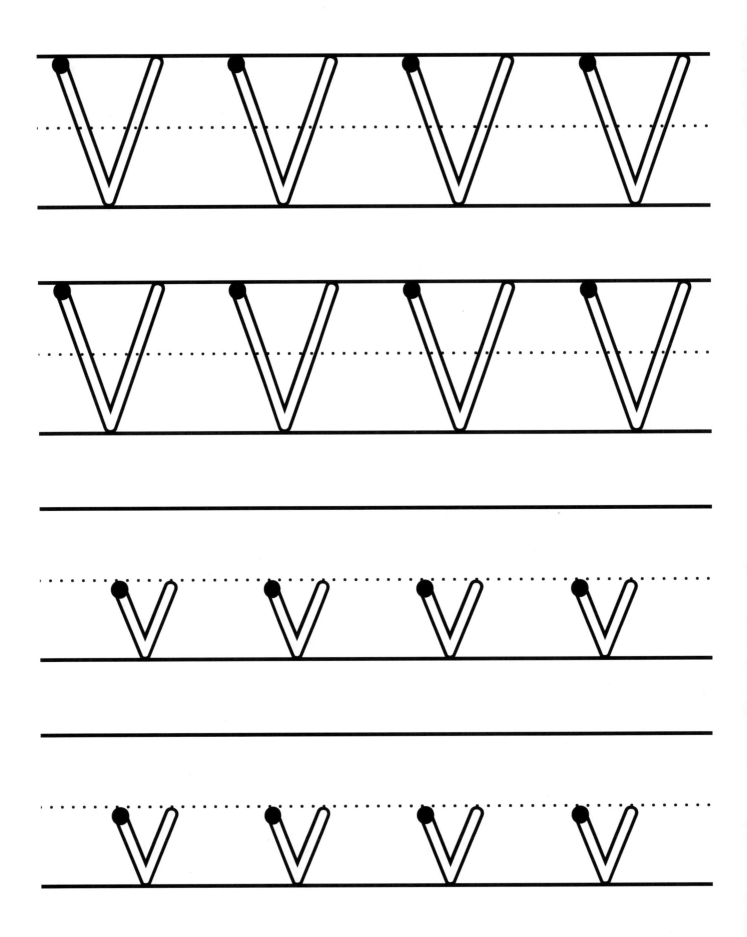

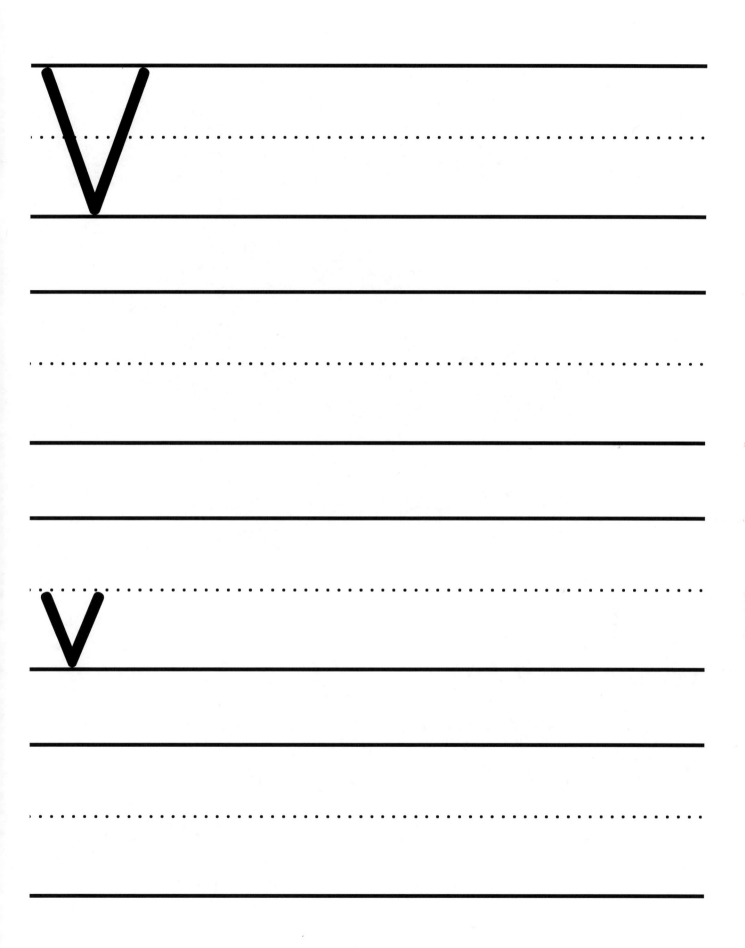

Whale

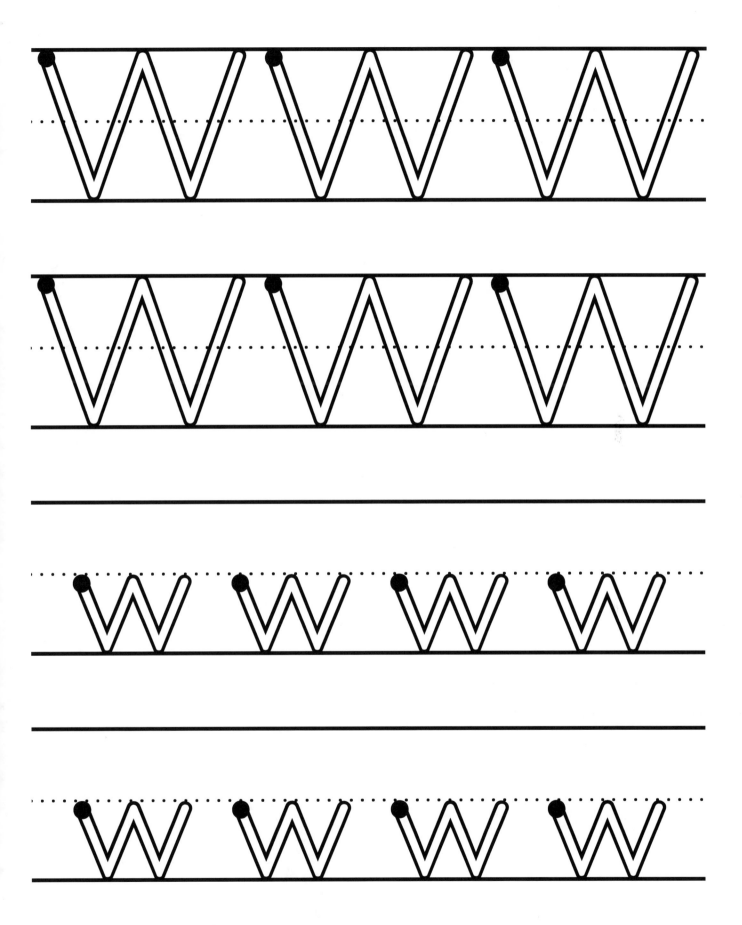

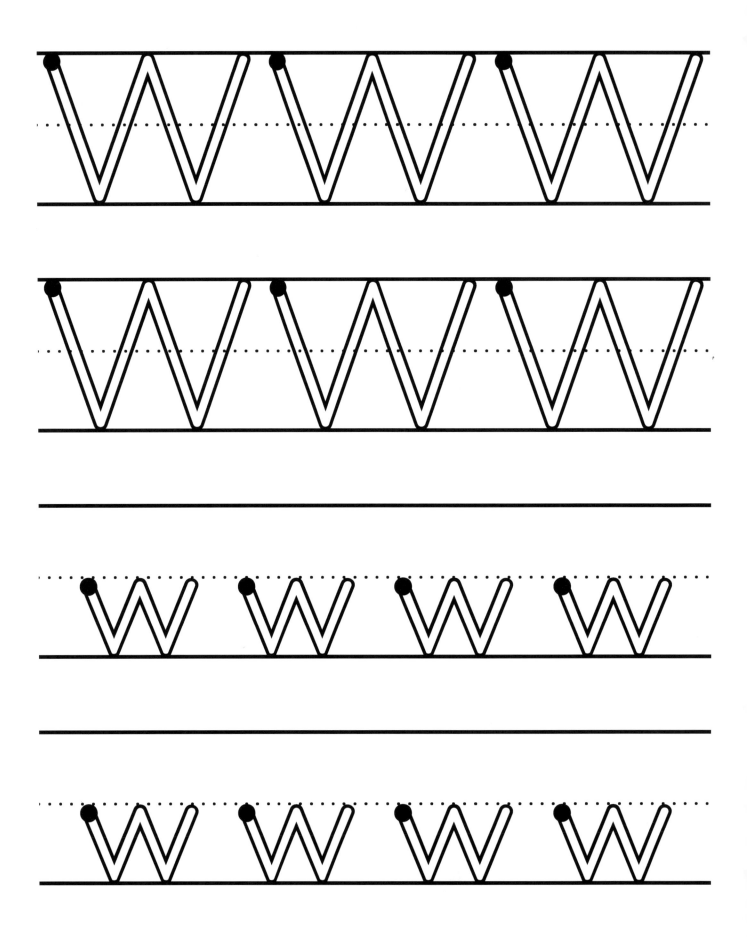

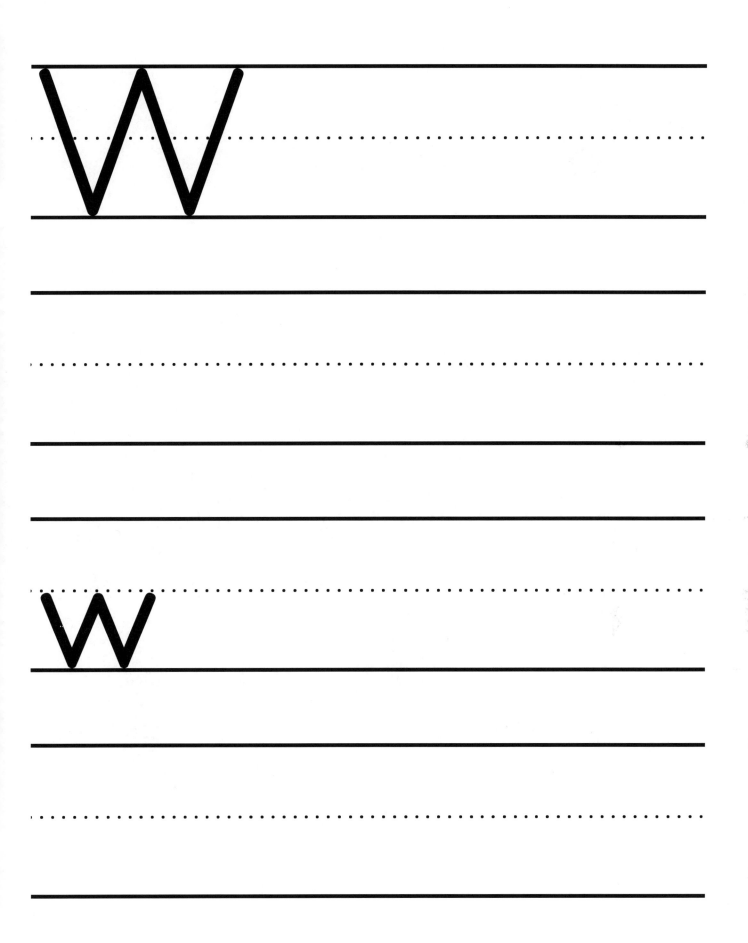

Xylophone

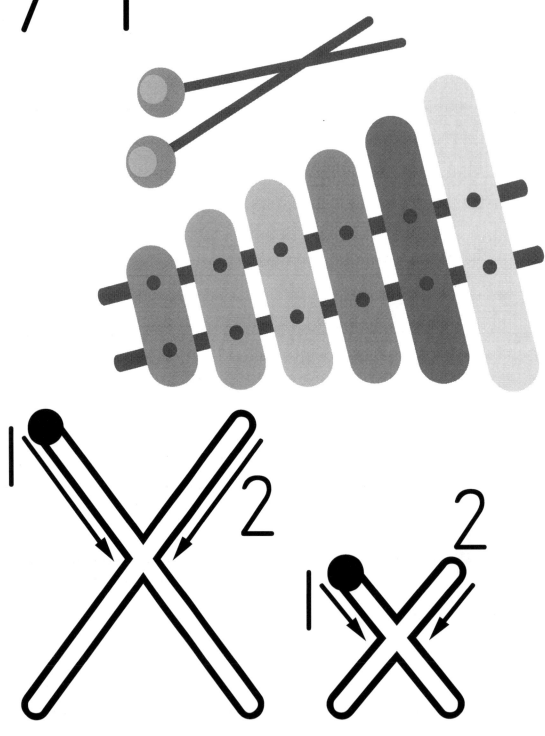

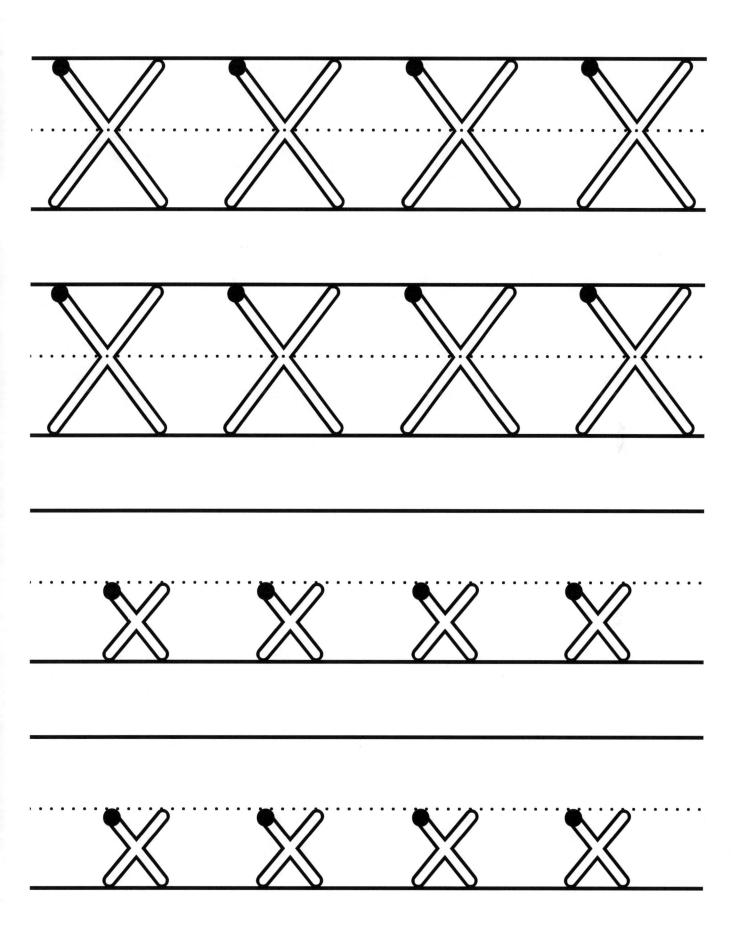

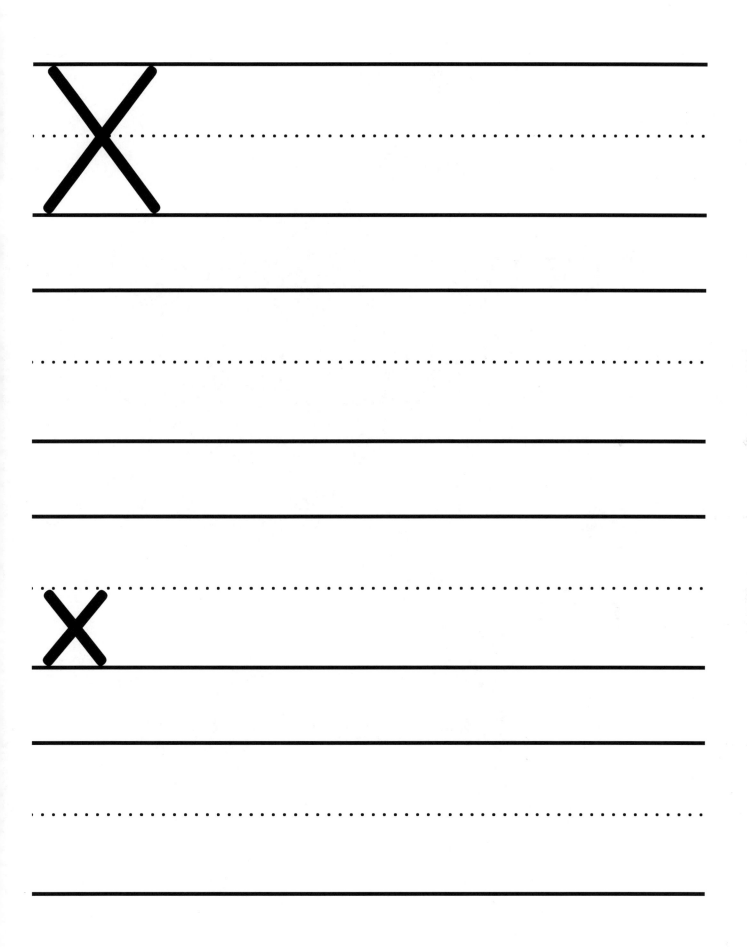

Yarn

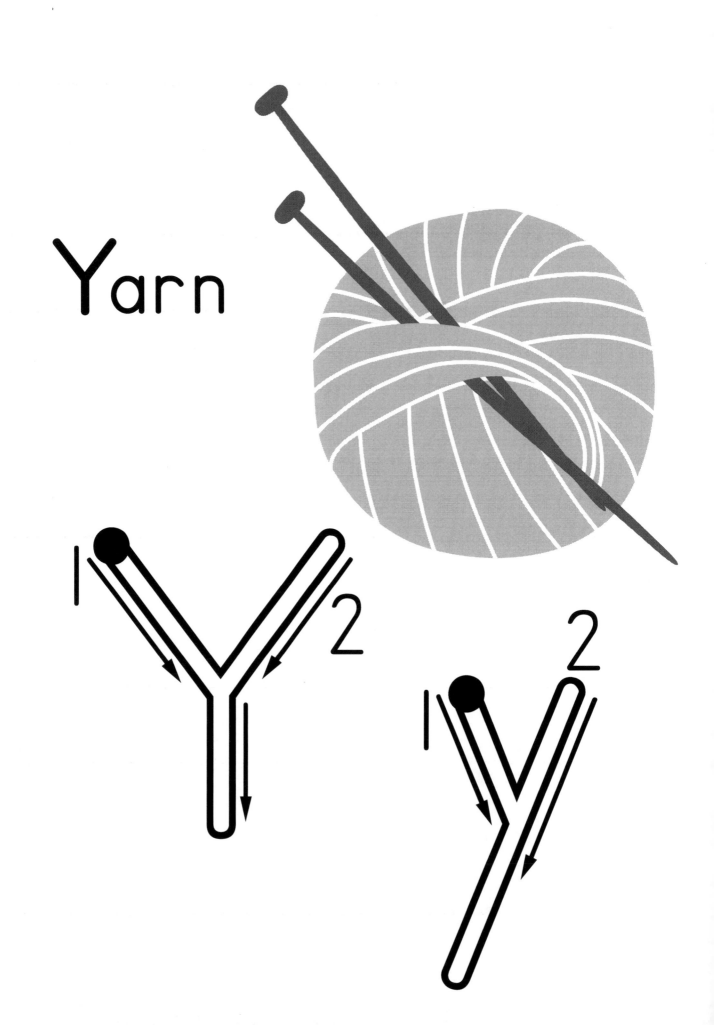

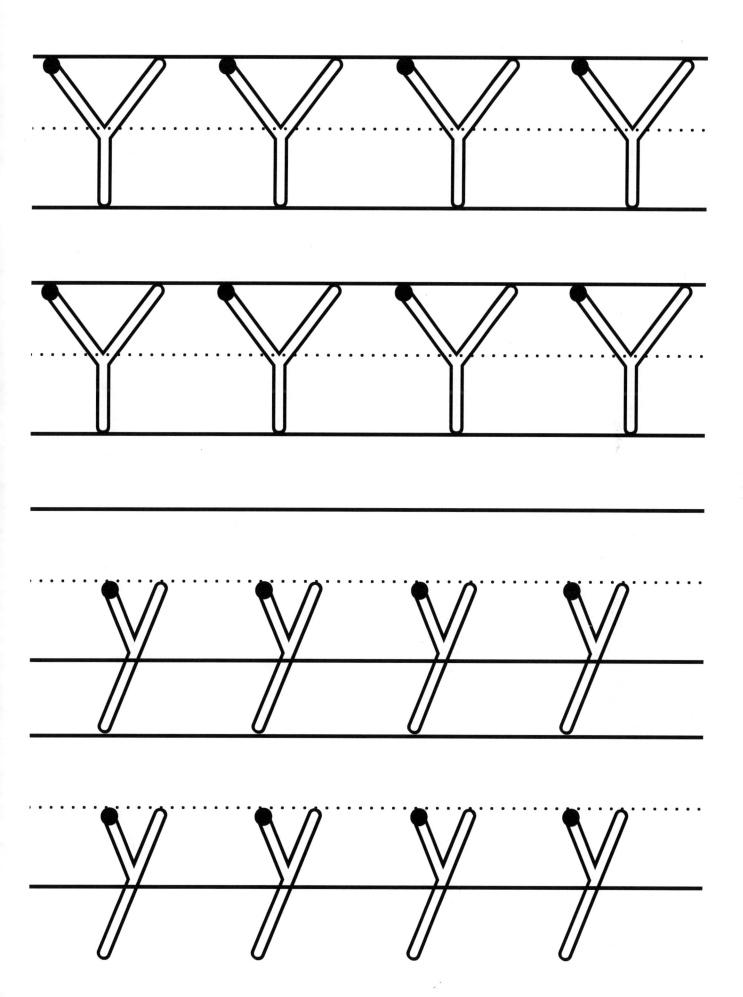

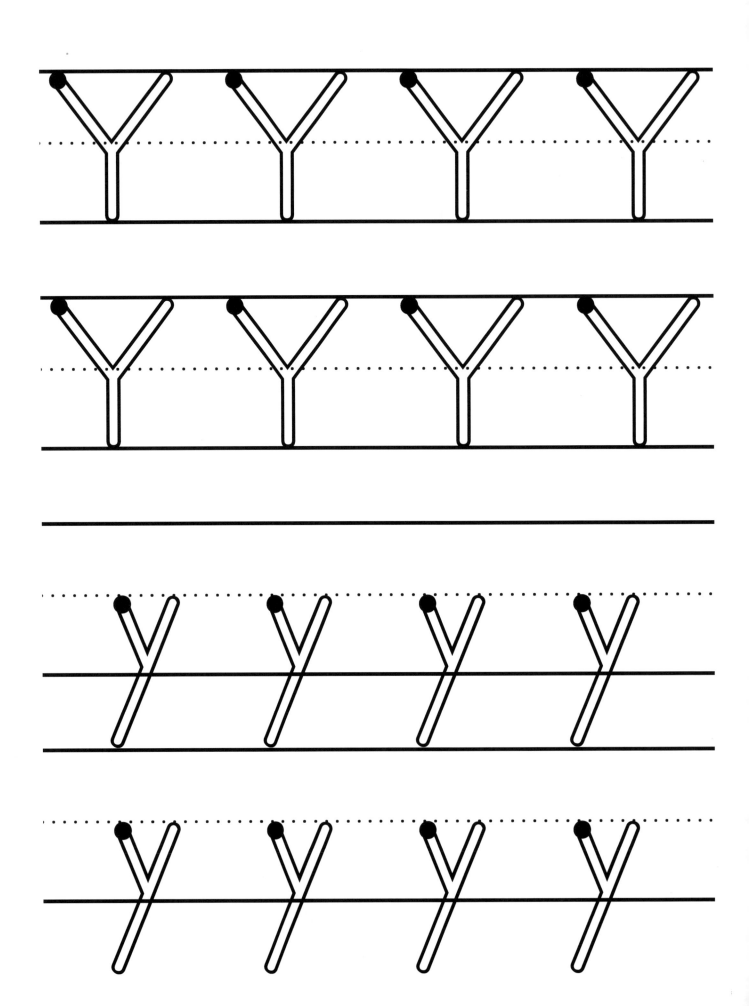

Y

y

Zebra

Z Z Z Z

Z Z Z Z

z z z z

z z z z

Z Z Z Z

Z Z Z Z

z z z z

z z z z

Z

z

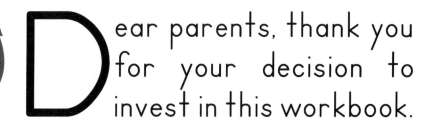

Dear parents, thank you for your decision to invest in this workbook.

If it meets your expectations, please **spare a minute to write a short review about it on Amazon.**

Your review will reward the efforts of our team, give us ideas for improvement and encourage us to create more workbooks that help children learn and practice new skills.

I truly thank you for your support.

Sincerely,

Victoria Vita

PS If you wish to send us feedback and comments, I would love to hear from you at my personal email address hellovictoriavita@gmail.com

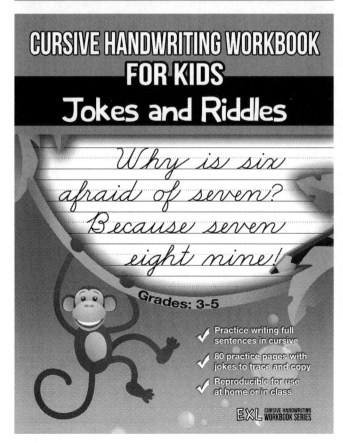

Made in the USA
Columbia, SC
12 February 2019